DRAGON FIRE

THE BATTLE

FOR

THE FALKLANDS

By Peter von Bleichert

D1520128

Books by Peter von Bleichert

Fiction

Crown Jewel: The Battle for the Falklands

Fourth Crisis: The Battle for Taiwan

Non-Fiction

Bleichert's Wire Ropeways

Blitz! Storming the Maginot Line

ACKNOWLEDGEMENTS

Thanks to my teachers: Jonathan E.; Bruce H.; Paul M.; Karen S.; and, Panayiotis Z.

And, a special thanks to: Robert N. (UK).

DEDICATION

Michael Muxie, III (in memoriam).

And, to those lost on both sides of the real Falklands War: 'Sleep well you Bonnie Lads/*Duerme bien valientes muchachos*.'

TABLE OF CONTENTS

CHARACTERS

ARGENTINE REPUBLIC:

Cabo Segundo (Corporal Second Class) Gaston 'Raton' Bersa

Teniente de Fragata (First Lieutenant) Santiago Ledesma

Capitán de Navío (Captain) Jaime Matias

...and, Doctor Waldemar Amsel; Ministro de Defensa (Minister of Defense) Juan Cruz Gomez; & Capitán de Fragata (Lieutenant Commander) Augusto Moreno.

UNITED KINGDOM:

Captain Lawrence Fryatt

Leading Seaman John Mcelaney

Lieutenant Commander Nigel Williams

...and, Ordinary Seaman Rodi Dando; Lieutenant Angus Lowry; & Lieutenant Seamus McLaughlin.

NOTES

A British Overseas Territory, the Falkland Islands are a stark, wind-ripped South Atlantic archipelago some 400 miles east of Argentina's Patagonian coast, and 850 miles north of the Antarctic Circle. Comprising East Falkland, West Falkland, and 778 smaller islands, the Falkland Islands are roughly the size of the American State of Connecticut—about half the size of the country of Wales—and the capital is in the port city of Stanley on East Falkland. Falklanders are primarily of British, Chilean, and St. Helenian descent.

BRIEFING

The Argentine Republic claims sovereignty over the Falkland Islands.

Called *Las Islas Malvinas* by Argentinians, the archipelago is viewed as part of the South Atlantic Department of the Province of Tierra del Fuego.

The United Kingdom has never recognized this claim.

Although Falklanders have expressed a clear preference to remain under British rule, in hopes of easing tensions during the 1960s, London engaged in talks with Argentine foreign missions. The talks, however, failed to reach any meaningful conclusion.

In the early 1980s, a ruthless dictatorship ruled Argentina. Accordingly, it suffered a crippling economic crisis. In an attempt to distract and unify its restive populace, Argentina initiated *Operación Rosario* on April 2, 1982, and invaded the Falklands.

Argentine forces outnumbered the British garrison 10-to-1. Resistance was rapidly subdued, and within hours, Argentine forces occupied Government House in Stanley—the Falklands' capital—and flew their flag over this symbol of British hegemony.

British Prime Minister Thatcher—dubbed the 'Iron Lady' by the Soviets—immediately denounced the invasion. She roused her military, organized and commenced Operation Corporate, and dispatched a Task Group to retake the islands.

After fierce air and naval battles, British forces landed on East Falkland. By mid-June of 1982, British marines and soldiers held the high ground around the capital city. Soon thereafter, the routed Argentine occupation forces surrendered.

Despite this clear-cut defeat, Argentina has continued to claim the South Atlantic archipelago as her own. In 1994, the Transitional Provisions of the Constitution of the Argentine Nation were amended, thereby alleging 'legitimate and everlasting sovereignty' over *Las Islas Malvinas*, South Georgia, and the Sandwich Islands, as well as the corresponding maritime and insular areas.

With this legislation, the capture of said territories became a permanent and unswayable objective of the Argentine people...

PROLOGUE: FLYING FISH

"Who hears the fishes when they cry?"—Henry David Thoreau

4 May 1982

Her Majesty's Ship *Sheffield* was the lead hull of the Royal Navy's premiere Type 42 guided-missile destroyers. Christened by Queen Elizabeth II in 1971, *Sheffield* was located south-east of the Falklands, patrolling the Total Exclusion Zone, an area within which Great Britain had promised to destroy any intruding Argentinian vessels. *Sheffield* was accompanied by HMS *Coventry* and *Glasgow*—also Type 42s—sailing to her north. Together, the three ships ran a radar picket for the Task Group. Aside

9

from these three ships, the Task Group was composed of the aircraft carriers *Hermes* and *Invincible*, the landing platform docks *Fearless* and *Intrepid*, several other destroyers, as well as various container ships, ferries, freighters, frigates, liners, logistic ships, patrol vessels, submarines, supply ships, tankers, trawlers, and tugs. Even an ice patrol ship—HMS *Endurance*—had been thrown into the mix. The group was on 'defense watch' routine and at 'air warning yellow' as, two days prior, a British nuclear attack submarine had sunk Argentina's cruiser, the *General Belgrano*. Retaliation was expected.

Hermes and *Invincible* had launched Sea Harriers on combat air patrol, and ahead of the steaming group, *Glasgow* and *Sheffield* swept the skies with their long-distance radars (*Coventry* was experiencing difficulties with hers).

◊◊◊◊

At 9:45 that morning, two Argentine Navy Super Étendards had departed Rio Grande, Tierra del Fuego. Each of the French-built strike aircraft carried a single Exocet AM39 anti-ship missile at the right wing hard point, with the long, heavy weapon counter-balanced by a fuel tank on the other side. Vectored out to sea, the Super Étendards met a Hercules tanker and topped-off their fuel. Then they headed for the last reported position of the British Task Group.

The Argentines also included Type 42s in their inventory, and had used them to practice missile runs. Using the British-made destroyers, their pilots had learned to 'pick the lobes' of the Type 42's elderly air-search radar. They would fly in low and listen for their cockpit radar warning to sound. Whenever it did, they would shed more altitude, and thusly became proficient at sneaking in without detection. This was how the two Super Étendards got within 40 miles of the Royal Navy's Task Group this day.

Glasgow got the first inkling that something was amiss when she got a brief, fleeting radar contact. She immediately put up chaff—a radar-deceiving cloud of aluminum needles—and reported in to the group's flagship, Hermes. Not long thereafter, the carrier Invincible got her own radar hit and vectored her airborne Sea Harriers—affectionately called 'Shars'—to investigate. When the Shars found nothing, the contacts were declared 'spurious' by the group's anti-air warfare commander. Meanwhile, with Sheffield on their nose, the two Argentine Super És sped in at near wave-top.

Sheffield's Operations Room was nestled deep in the destroyer's hull. This is where the Air Warfare Officer—the AWO—manned a radar display. Like the others huddled in the dimly-lit and cold room, he wore anti-flash gear composed of a white fire-resistant hood and elbow-length gloves. The AWO's partially masked face glowed yellow in the screen light as he watched the line sweep around the screen. When the radar's beam of radio waves struck something airborne and solid, it backscattered and boomeranged back, to be collected by the antenna mounted high on *Sheffield*'s superstructure. On the screen, the line came around again. This time, it revealed three blips.

The AWO knew that two of the blips represented friendly Sea Harriers, and the other a Sea King helicopter on a supply run. The AWO had been on duty for several hours, and his eyes blurred and itched. He took them off the screen, and dug his fingers in for a good scratch.

The two Argentine aircraft had closed to about 25 miles from the British warship. Both Super És climbed and turned on their Agave radars. The system energized, and found and locked on to *Sheffield*.

"*Blanco*," Lieutenant Commander Augusto Moreno, the pilot of the lead Super Étendard yelled as he used a hand signal to communicate with his wingman. Both men fed the data into their Exocet missiles.

Sheffield's AWO's radar line left two more blips on the screen. They were miles out and in a different quadrant than those known to represent friendly aircraft. When the AWO's tired focus returned, the blips had disappeared; this first chance for *Sheffield* to detect the stalking aircraft had been missed in a moment of human fatigue. Unfortunately for the Royal Navy destroyer and her company, a second opportunity was missed, as well.

At the same moment the Argentines had climbed to get a radar fix on *Sheffield*, the ship's captain contacted London by satellite. Perched high in the ship's mast was located an emitter warning antenna that would have detected the enemy's energy emission. However, *Sheffield*'s satellite communication system happened to use the same frequency band as that of the Super Étendards' radar. Therefore, as the destroyer's captain sent his reports home, the emitter warning antenna was deafened. With their Exocets locked-on and warmed up, the Argentine jets continued to charge on the oblivious British warship. The Super És again flew below the lobes of *Sheffield*'s radar.

"*Fuego*," Moreno said as he signaled by hand. Both pilots toggled their firing switches, and as the half-ton missiles dropped into the slipstream, both pilots counteracted the jarring force using ailerons.

The solid-propellant motors of both of the anti-ship missiles ignited, fire torching from their tail ends. The Exocets then settled in 12 feet above the calm, blue sea. Within seconds, they were moving at just beneath the speed of sound. Due to their cruise altitude and the curvature of the Earth, *Sheffield* remained blinded to their approach.

When the Argentine missiles were just six miles from *Sheffield*—less than 50 seconds from impact—the destroyer's AWO spotted the returns and announced: "Interim radar contact." The Operations Director strolled over and asked the AWO: "What've you got, then?"

On the screen, what had previously been a smudge of light, became two distinct blips. The Exocets were now 30 seconds away from *Sheffield*.

"Probable targets," the AWO shouted.

The Operations Director informed the Missile Director of the contact.

Twenty-five seconds…

The Missile Director queried the ship's Sea Dart surface-to-air missile fire control system.

Twenty seconds…

Along with the captain, the officers-of-the-watch and the rest of *Sheffield*'s bridge personnel, Sub-Lieutenant

Lawrence Fryatt kept a wary eye on the sea. A terrible feeling crept over Fryatt as he scanned his assigned quadrant of sea with binoculars. He spotted something, a puff of smoke on the horizon. Fryatt focused his binoculars there. The sea's surface shimmered within the black-edged circle of his view.

Torpedo? Fryatt wondered. He scrutinized the picture again and shifted his view upward. There, just above the diamonds of reflected sunlight, an airborne white cylinder skimmed above the waves. It was pointed right at him.

"Missile; terminal," Fryatt yelled at the very same moment the Action Information Center—the 'AIC,' or 'Op Room'—announced 'air warning red' over the bridge speaker. The captain raised his own binoculars and said, "Exocets," using the name as a curse.

Fryatt raised his binoculars again and found the second missile. He knew that the weapons were already inside the engagement envelope of *Sheffield*'s Sea Darts. *Anyway*, he thought, *Sea Darts are nearly useless against sea-skimmers.*

Sheffield's captain initiated a turn. Then he used the address system to order the ship's company to brace for missile impact before calling for 'damage control state 1.' With the ship already on 'defense watch, second readiness,' all watertight compartments had been sealed, and with less than five seconds to impact, there was no time to get chaff up and properly bloomed. Fryatt looked around. Most of the people were already on the floor and huddled together. Fryatt pressed the captain's shoulder to urge him to get down, but the captain pushed back. So, both men stood there, transfixed, and watched as the Exocets streaked in.

One Exocet malfunctioned. It wobbled, dipped, and slammed into the sea. The captain and Fryatt looked at one another and smiled. Their chances of surviving had just doubled. The smiles faded fast, however; as the remaining Exocet continued to home in. Time slowed for Fryatt. He even counted in his head: *Three, two, one…*

There was a blurred white streak, and then *Sheffield* lurched hard. The Exocet had pierced her amidships, just above the waterline, tearing a jagged gash in her side. The missile penetrated '2-Deck' at the Galley, killing several sailors instantly. The missile's momentum drove it into the Forward Auxiliary Machinery Room and the Forward Engine Room. The impact's shock wave buckled doors and collapsed ladders, and shrapnel tore the high-pressure fire main and ignited the diesel oil in the engine room ready tanks. The unspent missile propellant contributed thick black toxic smoke that suffocated personnel as it marched through compartment after compartment. *Sheffield* burned.

Fryatt had been knocked to the deck. He strained to rise. Achingly, he managed to do so and checked on the captain and the others that had been stationed around him. Fryatt then went to the fire-fighting system's control panel.

Water pressure warnings flashed. Fryatt manipulated switches as he tried desperately to restart the pumps. To his dismay, and despite numerous attempts, each section's pumps failed to restart. Then the panel flickered and went black as the bridge lost power. Fryatt opened the outer hatch and the bridge was instantly inundated with pungent smoke. He began to make his way aft.

Fryatt's feet felt warm. He looked down at his heavy standard-issue boots and saw their thick rubber soles sizzling on the deck. He looked around. The ship's grey paint had begun to peel from the superstructure as the steel warped. *There's an inferno inside.* Fryatt leaned over *Sheffield*'s gunwale. Heat smacked him in the face. Instinctively, he recoiled and raised his hands to protect himself. Fryatt's eyes stung from the acrid fumes created by burning fuel and plastics. Tears streaming, he blinked it off. Then he took a deep breath and held it, shielded his eyes with a hand, and leaned over the side. He again felt the high temperature. Though he could smell and feel the singing of his eyelashes and brows, he opened his eyes, and resisting the urge to close them and retreat, he managed to survey the damage.

He had seen the hole in *Sheffield*'s freeboard, and determined it to be about four by 15 feet. Its jagged edges glowed white hot and hissed steam every time the cold sea sloshed against it. In that moment, Fryatt concluded the Exocet had not detonated. He retreated and exhaled his held breath before gasping for cooler air.

"Damn," he said, and considered that, if the ship's company was able to control and extinguish the fires, *Sheffield* might just be saved. He turned, reached a hand out, and hesitantly tested the temperature of a hatch's latch.

It was warm and tolerable. He clasped his hand about it and opened the portal. Inside, he found only heat and thick, choking smoke. He pushed on into the blackened passageway. It was just several meters before his lungs demanded air. He tried to take a breath. The bite on his airway was harshly acrid and hot. His throat closed and he grabbed at it, trying again to breathe. His body denied his effort, and instead it folded over and slid down a wall. A fellow sailor wearing a respirator grabbed and pulled Fryatt back outside and into the open air. Fryatt immediately coughed and sucked in great breaths of air.

When his greedy breathing slowed again, and he was able to look up and concentrate, Fryatt saw a great grey wall beside *Sheffield*. It was the frigate *Yarmouth*. She had come alongside. Her hoses provided boundary cooling, and her sailors and small boats provided rescue. Though Fryatt repeatedly coughed and continued struggling to breathe, he managed to return a salute thrown from a sailor on *Yarmouth*'s deck.

Five hours later, *Sheffield* was abandoned to the fire. Her surviving crew had been transferred, and the proud warship's smoking, steaming hulk was left to roll and pitch on the cold, frothy sea. Two hours after that, flame roared from every one of *Sheffield*'s openings, and her steel bent and turned black with char. *Sheffield* fought her last battle there, upon the South Atlantic, and resisted the rot of flame for some six days. Then, with all the dignity she could muster, *Sheffield* succumbed, rolled onto her side, and went down. An hour later, she rested on the bottom being inspected by fish. Nineteen of her dead remained with her.

From *Hermes*' flight deck, yet another of *Sheffield*'s dead was tipped over the deck. He had perished, and was committed to the sea, in sure and certain hope of the Resurrection unto eternal life. Twenty-six more of

Sheffield's wounded suffered in the carrier's sick ward with burns, shock, and smoke inhalation. Sub-Lieutenant Lawrence Fryatt was among them.

Several decades later…

1: NAVIS

"Four hoarse blasts of a ship's whistle still raise the hair on my neck and set my feet to tapping."—John Steinbeck

The Norwegian Sea, a vast, black flatness, shivered in the cold, clear night. Pricks of bright light filled the sky and reflected in the calm water. These stars made it hard to tell where the heavens ended and the sea began. They seemed to be alive and spoke to one another with staccato flickers. A lone warship made way upon the sea, disturbing the black diamond-sprinkled tapestry, cleaving and pushing aside the reflected stars in a wave that undulated across the ocean's surface.

This warship was His Majesty's Ship *Dragon*, the Royal Navy's latest guided-missile destroyer. Of the *Daring*-class, otherwise known as the Type 45, *Dragon* was some 500 feet-long and crowned by a towering pyramidal mast topped by a radar dome. Like her namesake, *Dragon* had deadly sharp claws and teeth.

A floating fortress, *Dragon*'s archers were missiles; her catapults: guns; and Merlin lived in a cave at her stern. *Dragon* wore an invisibility cloak of sorts, with faceted sides that scattered enemy radar waves from her deceptive grey form. Every bit the agile slippery wyrm, this proud ship could examine air, sea, and space in crystal screens, and when cornered or when in the mood, she could breathe fire. Like most castles of old, just one man ruled this floating realm.

Dragon's bridge served as Captain Lawrence Fryatt's throne room. Surrounded by loyal and obedient lieges,

Fryatt exercised well-earned authority from a barely cushioned cold metal chair. Though his voice was often soft, sometimes even whispered, it thundered nonetheless. His voice brought immediate compliance, driving actions that were frequently a matter of life or death.

Like most in the Royal Navy, Fryatt was a simple man; he believed in country, duty, monarch, and navy. He also believed that the Type 45s, with their Sea Viper primary anti-air missile system, stood alone as the world's premiere anti-air warfare surface vessels. *The Americans could keep their Aegis cruisers*, Fryatt thought; *the Chinese could parade their Type 054A frigates all they wanted; and, the Russians could stuff their Project 21956 destroyers*. Fryatt was proud of *Dragon*, proud of those he commanded, and he possessed an unwavering commitment to defense of the realm. Captain Fryatt adjusted his collar and shifted in his chair.

It's too hot, Fryatt thought. Ever since fighting the blaze aboard *Sheffield*, ever since seeing the burned men, Fryatt had hated excessive heat. Even though the ship's environmental system was doing its job of keeping the bridge and its company snug, the warm, dry breeze made Fryatt fidgety. He stood, drawing a concerned look from the officer-of-the-watch, a man who tried to anticipate his captain's every need. Fryatt made his way to an exterior hatch. He swung open the heavy portal, and uttered a single word to whomever could hear: "Tea." He stepped out to the bridge wing.

Fryatt clanged the hatch shut. Although the steel door could ward off biological agents, chemicals, and radiation, he used it to keep his company at bay—to steal a moment in a place that otherwise did not allow much privacy. While he accepted the strong steaming mug of lemon-tinged Earl Grey that arrived within moments, Fryatt would tolerate no other disturbances. He went to the rail and leaned upon it. It propped up his tired body. The rail also transmitted the ship's harmonic to Fryatt's bones.

Dragon's bow gently rose and fell as she plowed through the sea, kicking up a spray that turned frosty and sparkled in the starlight. Fryatt drew a sharp, frigid breath that stung his lungs. He exhaled it as a cloud, watched it get caught in the breeze, and recalled his grandfather.

Fryatt's grandfather had sailed the Murmansk Run during the Second World War, the run that brought supplies to a choked Soviet Union. The man had sailed an old steam merchant over these very waters, had skirted U-boats and the feared convoy raider *Tirpitz*, as well as icebergs that calved from the jagged shores of Greenland and became caught up in the Eastern Icelandic current. Fryatt sipped his tea and pondered the throbbing stars blanketing the dark night.

Fryatt had grown up in the west-end of London, a place where the night sky had for centuries been polluted with artificial light, light that subdued the glowing ribbon of the Milky Way, dulling its wonder. Tonight, however, far from the influence of man's cityscapes, Earth and sky were beheld as they were meant to be: a vision that begged questions and forced fundamental things to be asked, private thoughts like: 'Who am I?' and 'Why am I here?' Despite such existential considerations, Fryatt knew why he, his comrades, and His Majesty's warship were here, at the top of the world.

Russia had reawakened; the bear roused by a leader longing for empire. This leader had turned back time and progress, back to when east and west stood eye-to-eye and toe-to-toe. Flush with oily cash, the Russian had claimed most of the Arctic, and, in support of these aspirations, the Russian Federation had built new attack subs and missile boats. These machines and their men stretched their legs and made the Greenland-Iceland-UK Gap come alive again. Furthermore, resurrected strategic bombers—Backfires and Bears—once again flew out of the Kola Peninsula to buzz the Finns, Swedes and Norwegians, and play chicken with the United Kingdom's northern air defense identification zone.

While the Royal Air Force gave its own unique brand of hell to such unwelcome visitors, *Dragon* and her sisters also reminded the Russian bombers that, like during the Cold War, they were not wanted in this part of the neighborhood. Intelligence, as well as over-the-horizon radar stations in Scotland, told the Royal Navy what was headed their way. This was how Fryatt knew he could expect airborne company tonight, in fact within the hour. In the meantime, however, he was content to cherish the star-lit Arctic night.

Fryatt raised his dominant hand to the sky. It was the left one. He waved the square of his palm about, half-expecting the protuberances of his fingers to displace the stars, to push them along into streaks of lights, to wash them around like glitter that floated in black ink. Despite the grin on his face and this moment of suspended reality, Fryatt failed to influence the canvas of night, and in the end, remained as inconsequential as he had expected to be. However, when a sailor burst through the bridge hatch and announced that the ship's Action Information Center had an airborne radar contact, Fryatt knew that, at the very least, he could affect terrestrial events. He could influence the behavior of his fellow humans. He took one last draw of the sharp air. It reminded him he was alive, and, it reminded him he wanted to stay that way.

"Captain on the bridge," was announced as Fryatt re-entered the warm enclosure. Fryatt always loved the sound of those four words. Just a lad from Hounslow, he still felt a rush as highly-qualified uniformed people acknowledged his presence, straightened their stance, and raised their chins. His thoughts turned to that of his charge—his ship.

The vibration of *Dragon*'s bridge deck spoke to him. It said that the ship was slicing through the water at some 25 knots. Deep in the hull, *Dragon*'s twin gas turbines and diesel generators thumped away. Fryatt felt them provide power to the electric motors, which in turn sent 27,000 horsepower to the shafts. Two propellers translated this power to the water, cutting it, grabbing it, and pushing it away. Going to his chair, Fryatt ran his hands over the bridge control panel. He dragged each finger across the hard knobs and soft rubber-covered buttons. *A ship is like a familiar lover*, he pondered. As her tremble was felt, one adjusted touch to achieve harmonious vibration, to take her in the right direction, to bring her where she wanted, where she longed, to go. Fryatt sat down in his chair. It, too, vibrated. He smiled as *Dragon* hummed happily along.

Lieutenant-Commander Nigel Williams—*Dragon*'s second-in-command and one of 190 souls aboard—peered at a terminal. Bathed in its green glow, Williams' eyes squinted, his jaw set. Then he turned to the captain.

"Sir, the ship is at 'air warning yellow,'" telling the captain that his men and women were ready for trouble.

"Lovely night," the captain responded, acknowledging the information while maintaining his façade of unflappability.

"It is."

A bell rang. Williams spun around again to check another screen.

"Flash. Op Room reports airborne contacts," Williams announced.

"Right," the captain said with a glance to the clock. "Our Russian friends are right on time. Bring the ship to 'air warning red.' Maintain speed and course."

Williams acknowledged and brought the ship to action stations.

Dragon's dimly lit Op Room was cold. Despite the heaters, the icy Norwegian Sea reached through the hull and chilled the bones of the sailors manning rows of computer terminals and radar screens. One of these sailors energized the SAMPSON 3-D multifunction phased-array radar perched high atop *Dragon*'s forward mast. It fired beams through the atmosphere and found two low-altitude targets, populating the Op Room's screens with blips and numbers.

"Flag, AWO, probable targets. Two tracks inbound at two-seven-five degrees. Altitude: 3,000 feet. Speed: Mach zero-point-nine." The numbers beside the radar blips changed. "Tracks have accelerated. Now at Mach one-point-one. They've gone supersonic. Flight profile suggests Russian Backfire bombers."

The Tu-22M Backfire was a swing-wing, long-range strategic and maritime strike bomber. Its two giant Kuznetsov NK-25 turbofans pushed the big bomber to Mach 1.88. When not on nuclear patrol, Backfires usually left base with a load of long-range anti-ship missiles; likely the older, though effective, AS-4 Kitchens; or worse for *Dragon*, newer SS-N-22 Sunburns.

"Radar warning," a sailor yelled out. The Backfires had energized their Down Beat missile targeting radar and painted *Dragon* with energy. Though *Dragon*'s sloped sides, faceted mast and radar-absorbent material inhibited the Backfire's ability to lock on, the closer the airplanes got, the higher their chance of a successful missile launch. The Russian bombers drove in hard and fast.

"Jam their signal," Captain Fryatt ordered. Though he knew the Russians were unlikely to fire, he would play the game by the rules anyway and try to send them home with bruised egos. From the top of *Dragon*'s main mast, the integrated intercept and jammer suite's antenna began to transmit at the same wavelength as the Backfires' radar. If all went as advertised, an electronic fog had spread across the Backfire's cockpit screen, temporarily concealing *Dragon*'s movements. Fryatt ordered a hard turn to port. The ship's company braced against the lean of the deck. "Shoot them down," Fryatt told Williams with a cheeky grin.

Williams smiled back. As they had discussed previously, *Dragon* would use the intruders to conduct an exercise. Williams picked up the VUU—the ship's Voice User Unit—and told the AIC to run an Aster missile drill. The ship's phased-array radar fired a targeting beam into the face of the two Backfires. A Klaxon sounded aboard

Dragon. It warned the ship's company to stay away from

the Sylver A-50 vertical launch system, an array of 48

missile cells sunk into the ship's forward deck. Inside each

cell hid a dart-shaped Aster surface-to-air missile.

The Aster series could engage and take down aircraft,

cruise missiles and ballistic missiles. *Right now, the*

Russian's cockpit warning panels must be lit up like a

Christmas tree, Fryatt thought. *They know that the tables*

have been turned, that they had been detected, were being

targeted, and should I so desire, supersonic missiles would

soon be on the way to rip into their fuselage and wings.

Fryatt stood, went to the windscreen, and peered out at

Dragon's forward deck.

Had the captain authorized release of weapons, two

Asters would have blasted open their frangible cell covers,

erupted from the deck in a fountain of fire, and raced off to meet the Backfires. Op Room announced the radar contacts had climbed, slowed, and turned around.

"Well, that was fun," Fryatt said to the bridge crew. They all chuckled and nodded. "Bring us back to patrol course and reduce speed to 18 knots. Stand down from air warning red and revert to yellow."

Several minutes later Captain Fryatt was in his cabin reading and eating a sandwich. He heard a knock at the door.

"Come," Fryatt said. The wood-paneled door slid open. It was Lieutenant-Commander Williams, carrying a print-out. He asked forgiveness for the disturbance, handed his Captain the paper, and retreated again to the passageway. Fryatt rubbed his eyes, unfolded the decrypted message, and began to read:

PROTECTIVELY MARKED INFORMATION

ENCRYPTION KEY: ATD3GW

FR: NAVY COMMAND HEADQUARTERS

TO: HMS DRAGON

REPUBLIC OF ARGENTINA (ROA) HAS

INVADED/HOLDS SOUTH ATLANTIC OVERSEAS

TERRITORY OF FALKLAND ISLANDS. STATE OF

WAR EXISTS WITH ROA.

ORDERS:

RENDEVOUS WITH HMS IRON DUKE AT 8S 14W

PROCEED IN UNISON AT BEST SPEED TO 51S 54W

AND RENDEVOUS WITH HMS AMBUSH

RULES OF ENGAGEMENT ULTRA—ENGAGE AND

DESTROY ALL ENEMY CONTACTS. PROVIDE

THEATRE–WIDE ANTI-AIR WARFARE UMBRELLA

FOR FRIENDLY FORCES

END TRANSMISSION

Fryatt remembered having read that the Crown Prince had been headed to the Falklands for a tour. He thought of his old ship, *Sheffield*, and remembered the agonized groans of the badly burned man that had lain beside him in *Hermes'* sick ward. He thought about the AM39 Exocet.

During the 1982 Falklands War, other than sinking *Sheffield*, Exocet had damaged the merchant ship *Atlantic Conveyor*, and set the destroyer *Glamorgan* ablaze. Fryatt knew that Argentina now had over 200 Exocets in inventory, including the latest MM40 Block 3 version. While he knew that *Dragon* was far better equipped to handle this menace than *Sheffield* had been, he also knew that these weapons would be their greatest nightmare. What had not crossed his mind, however, was the fact of Argentina's new submarines.

2: ABISMO

"They say the sea is cold, but the sea contains the hottest blood of all…"—D.H. Lawrence

There were strange snaps, clicks, and haunting songs. The trio of sound was layered over a bass section of low-frequency groans. This orchestra of life belonged to the Atlantic Ocean, and, from the murk beneath the waves, another sound grew louder, rhythmic and unnatural. A shadow approached. It was blacker than the blackness.

Argentine submarine ARA *San Luis II* was a Project 877EKM Paltus diesel-electric attack submarine, better known by the NATO designation of Kilo. Paltus meant Halibut, and, like the large bottom-dwelling flatfish, *San*

Luis II could blend in, conceal herself, and lay in wait to snap up unwary prey. Built in Nizhniy Novgorod, Russia, like most things made there, the submarine had been sold like a drug in a dark alley. Cold cash had sealed the deal. Yes, to some on Argentina's Cabinet of Ministers, a submarine was just a steel hole in the water that did not feed people, plow fields, sow seeds, nor provide shelter to the poor. But to others, *San Luis II* represented a means to an end, and existed, therefore, as a beautiful thing.

San Luis II—called, simply, *Numero Dos* (Number Two) by her crew—featured a hemispheric bow that housed sonar and six big weapon tubes for mines, missiles, and torpedoes. She bore dive planes just forward of a large sail emblazoned with the big white pennant number 'S-44.' Antennae, two periscopes and a snorkel through which the diesels breathed, jutted from the sail's top. The submarine's fat and stubby, stretched teardrop-shaped, hull ended with a lower stabilizer fin/rudder and a single big six-bladed propeller. As to a blind man, sound was *San Luis II*'s eyes.

She towed behind her a microphone-covered wire and, mounted hull-side, was the Rubikon passive sonar array. These 'eyes' collected sounds from the water, and allowed *San Luis II* to see in the dark. Her speed increased, and then she reeled in her towed array. Within the pressure hull, beyond the reach of the great crush of ocean, is where *San Luis II*'s human operators existed. They dwelt in a tangled thicket of pipes and valves that lined a claustrophobes' nightmare of artificial caves, grottoes, hatches, and tubular tunnels. The sonar station occupied a small space just off the main Control Room.

This is where sounds were filtered and analyzed by computers and their sophisticated software. The computers then presented the sounds to technicians. A glowing screen, one of many, displayed graphical bars that cascaded like a waterfall. Each bar represented bearing, frequency, and the range of sonar contacts. The sonar technician pointed to one such bar and asked what he was listening to: "*¿Que es eso?*"

"Whales screwing," the senior sonar technician answered. The accent revealed a youth spent in the mountainous north-western Argentinian province of Catamarca.

"And that background noise?" the subordinate added.

"That, my friend, is from tectonic plates; the Mid-Atlantic Ridge. The crackle you hear, just like your breakfast cereal?"

"Yes."

"That is lava flash-cooling in seawater."

The tech nodded understanding, but his slackened jaw revealed lingering confusion coupled with fascination.

The senior sonar technician pressed his headphones tighter to his ears and stated: "We are never going to hear anything at this speed." *San Luis II*'s diesel generators continued throbbing away, masking the subtle sounds that could represent another submarine.

San Luis II was on a north-easterly speed course, her depth now ten meters beneath the surface of the ocean, that undulating membrane between air and water. The sub's diesels breathed through a snorkel that ripped the water like a shark's fin, sucking vital oxygen that all Earth-bound creatures need, even those made of metal. The invasion of the Falklands—*Operación Maza*—was underway, and *San Luis II* would do her part. She arrived on station just 40 minutes behind schedule.

Captain Jaime Matias, *San Luis II*'s commander, sat at the small fold-down desk shoehorned into a corner of his quarters. Unlike the rest of the boat's lime-green painted metal walls, this tiny room was wood-paneled and offered a private bed. *San Luis II*'s other crewmen had to share bunks, with one man waking to go on duty, and the other jumping in as he came off it. Captain Matias' bed was not quite as long as he was tall, its mattress was cracker-thin, and it was tucked against the slope of the hull. Although it felt like crawling into a coffin, it was nevertheless cool and clean. Even better, it was all his.

Matias looked to the three small, framed portraits hanging on the cabin wall. They had been affixed there in the yard, forcing the commander to bear the unblinking gazes of President Alonso, Admiral Correa, and Minister of Defense Gomez. Matias sighed, stood, and hung a towel over the portraits. He sat again and pulled a cozy off a small pot that had been delivered by the cook and poured himself a mug of *yerba maté*—a bitter, earthy green tea. Then he picked up the small picture of his wife and son from his desk.

Matias sipped the tea and looked closely at his boy. He, too, wore the uniform of the Argentine Navy, and had he lived, he would be an officer by now. There was a knock at the door.

"Come."

It was First Lieutenant Santiago Ledesma, *San Luis II*'s executive officer.

"Pardon the interruption, sir," Ledesma said as he peeked in.

"Enter, Santiago," the captain invited. "Sit." Ledesma squeezed in, sat on the bed, and accepted a mug which Matias filled with tea.

"Thank you, sir." Ledesma blew at the steaming brew and took a sip. "Sir, we are at 13 south 17 west, the edge of our patrol sector."

"Very well," Matias said. *San Luis II*'s endurance had been pushed as she steamed some 3,000 miles from base at

Mar del Plata, and now it was time for Matias to take the conn. With limited fresh water aboard and the extended duration of *San Luis II*'s mission, the boat's shower had been padlocked shut, and the combined odor of sweat and diesel oil recirculated through the ventilators. Feeling ripe, Matias changed his disposable shirt and splashed water on his face from the soup bowl-sized cabin basin. He pulled the towel down to dry himself, and then replaced it over the faces of his leaders. Ledesma chuckled.

"That is all they are good for, Santiago: A towel hook," Matias declared, and studied his executive's face. "Does this bother you?"

"This is your cabin. And we are friends."

"Then you can tell me how you really feel."

"Very well. Sometimes I am afraid of you. Sometimes I do not understand you. And sometimes, I am unsure if we really are friends."

"Oh, is that all?" Matias chuckled, but he appreciated the easy forthrightness of Ledesma. This was one of the reasons he had recommended the man as second-in-command. Ledesma sipped at his tea and peered at the captain through the wisps of steam rising from the mug.

"We *are* friends, Santiago. And, because of this, I will tell you something: This war is a mistake."

Though Ledesma harbored such forbidden thoughts as well, he was not prepared to discuss them, so he changed the subject.

"That is your son?" he asked.

"Once, I went to sea with a fresh heart. That was long ago," Matias added, studying Ledesma. Then Matias took the new path of conversation Ledesma had initiated: "Yes, that is my son. I taught him to be a good warrior: country, duty, ask no questions. Now he's at the bottom of the sea."

Ledesma had heard the story. When Argentina had hastily announced a nuclear submarine program and cobbled together a prototype based on a German TR-1700 hull, young submariners had paid the price. The program was abandoned when the contaminated boat and the radiation-burned bodies trapped within had been committed to the deep.

"Young and with faith... That is the way for a warrior to die, Santiago. I have lived too long." Matias could see he had said too much. "Don't worry, my friend. I am too well trained for such thoughts to interfere with my duty to you, our crew, and this wonderful boat." Matias touched a cold steel pipe over his head."

Ledesma nodded, forced a smile, and stood. "Thank you for the tea," he said. "I shall return to my post now."

"I am right behind you," Matias said with a smile. He watched Ledesma leave the confines of the cabin, and as the door shut, his forced smile quickly faded.

◊◊◊◊

Captain Matias ducked into the submarine's cramped Control Room. Like the rest of the sub, the Control Room was a tangle of analog dials, computers, electrical panels, levers, pipes, valves, and wire conduit covered by too many layers of paint. Red light illuminated the room, because except for clocks, interior lighting was the only indication of the time of day. Red lighting meant it was nighttime topside. Despite the dimness, Matias knew the location of every head-knocking low pipe and maneuvered accordingly. He passed dive control with its bank of valves and glowing control panels.

"Good evening, men," Matias said to the shadows hunched all along the compartment's wall. He quickly surveyed various analog and digital instruments arrayed around the Control Room. "Batteries?"

"Are at 100 percent, sir," Ledesma reported. They had been on diesel power for some time, charging the submarine's two banks of 120-cell lead-acid batteries.

"Excellent," Matias said. "Shut down the generators, stow the snorkel, and engage the electric motor."

"*Si, señor,*" Ledesma responded, and then repeated the order to the chief-of-the-boat. The slightly overweight chief made it all happen. The racket that had filled their ears for days went quiet, replaced by the sound of water in pipes, the occasional cough or sniffle, the manipulation of switches, and the gentle hum of electric propulsion. As Matias watched his crew at work, he hoped an aircraft, satellite, or surface vessel had not spotted the wake of *San Luis II*'s snorkel. He rationalized that the rough sea-state topside had likely obscured the snorkel's telltale signature.

He found comfort in the fact that, on batteries again, *San Luis II* was nearly silent and invisible.

"Make your depth 125 meters," Matias announced. Ledesma, and then the chief-of-the-boat, repeated the order. Valves were opened, panel indicators changed colors, and there was the sound of rushing water. The Control Room deck pitched forward as the submarine angled nose down, piercing the deep, dark depths.

The hull groaned and popped as its high-tensile steel adjusted to increased pressure. The greener submariners looked about nervously as this happened, while Matias and the Control Room's other experienced crew paid the sounds no mind. A drawn out creak made one man wriggle. Matias smiled at Ledesma who turned away to check a display. A loud bang announced the hull's adjustment to the squeeze of the Atlantic.

"You know..." Matias said to Ledesma, though he was really addressing all those present. "These boats are better than the old S-boats we used to ride to sea." Matias spoke of the dated Type 209's, the diesel submarines on which he had cut his teeth. "Those boats, like the first *San Luis*, made a racket like the whole ocean was rushing in. These are better." Though he knew Russian welders were known to cut corners, and that quality control on exported hulls was scant at best, he suppressed his own lingering doubts about the machine that had, so far, kept them alive. Matias put on a brave face and rocked on his heels.

"One hundred twenty-five meters, sir," Ledesma reported.

"Planes to zero degrees. Level us off."

In a small alcove off the Control Room, a band appeared on a monitor's sonar waterfall.

"Contact," the sonar technician announced. "Distant. On the surface. It's closing."

"Classify," Matias ordered in response.

"Range: four miles. Bearing: one-nine-zero degrees. Speed: 20 knots. I hear two propellers. High speed shafts. Not a merchantman. Computer is working on--" The clatter of a printer interrupted as it began to spit out a report. The sonar supervisor ripped off the paper it produced and read it aloud:

"Type 23 frigate. United Kingdom. *Duke*-class."

"Good. Our first catch of the day," Matias said with a greedy smile. Reassured by his captain's lust for the hunt, Ledesma grinned back. Then he opened a binder and began to read:

"Type 23. Thirty-six hundred tons. A top speed of 28 knots. Thales Type 2050NE bow-mounted sonar operating in the 4.5-7.5 kilohertz range, and a Dowty Type 2087 very low frequency towed array."

"Anti-submarine armaments?"

"Stingray torpedoes and a Merlin helicopter. Depending on her hull number, she could be carrying the SSTD torpedo countermeasures system." Ledesma scanned the rest of the binder's page. "The type is decommissioning; being replaced with a new class, the Global Combat Ship."

Matias looked to the weapons status board. *San Luis II* had wire-guided torpedoes in the two outer tubes, and wake-followers—53-65KEs—in the other four.

"What do you think, Santiago?" Matias asked Ledesma in a near whisper.

"The British would never expect us to be this far north."

Matias nodded agreement. When Admiral Correa had assembled his top naval officers to review plans, it was

Matias who had argued against deploying Argentina's best submarines in the waters surrounding *Las Islas Malvinas*. Instead, he pressed, they should be used to take the fight to the British, and not wait for them to come to the fight. Furthermore, he argued, the highly-capable and deeply-feared British nuclear submarines would likely deploy to and roam the war zone, making it the last place where the Argentine Navy should concentrate their valuable boats.

"That frigate is running too fast to have her towed array in the water. I would say she is sprinting south, and her captain is not expecting any interference just yet," Ledesma added. Matias smiled.

"Yes, Santiago. I concur. Creep us abeam of her. And bring us to battle stations."

3: DUKES UP

"The art of war is simple enough: Find out where the enemy is; Get at him as soon as you can; Strike at him as hard as you can and as often as you can, and keep moving on."—Ulysses S. Grant

The storm pushed the sea into tall wind-whipped peaks, cliffs of water that dropped off sharply into deep troughs. The water was dark, a deep purple, and rafts of froth rose and fell with the sloshing surface. A torrent of rain pelted HMS *Iron Duke* as her long, thin, grey hull rose and slammed back down, her stern corkscrewing and exposing her red underbelly and the tips of her shiny propellers. As the water piled up and folded over, the frigate's bridge crew stabbed the warship's bow through the waves' white crowns at the proper angle, thereby allowing maintenance of a decent speed.

"Five degrees starboard," the officer-of-the-watch yelled above the screaming wind and splashing water. *Iron Duke* turned to the right a bit more, rose steeply, rolled some, and then slammed back down in a surge of water and sea spray, momentarily submerging the bridge. The windshield's clear view screens—small round discs that spun to rapidly shed water—threw the water away as the ship's bow came back up and the cold seawater rushed away in a mass of green foam. The bow, supplemented by the buoyancy of the bulbous stem that contained the sonar, climbed again and scaled the next oceanic hill. Though *Iron Duke*'s Artisan 3D radar swept the area, the screens in the Operations Room were so full of clutter from wave crests that the radar operator could not discern the black pipe peeking from the depths.

San Luis II's periscope pierced the surface. Its lens surveyed the area before it disappeared again, swallowed by the rhythmic rise and fall of waves. Twenty feet below this protuberance, the black shadow of the Argentine submarine hovered steadily below the squall-battered surface. In the red glow of *San Luis II*'s Control Room's nighttime lighting, Captain Matias looked through the periscope's monocular eyepiece.

Matias spotted the green glow of *Iron Duke*'s bank of bridge windows and the powerful flashlight of a deckhand scurrying along the rail, checking for storm damage. Matias waited for the next wave to pass. Bubbles cleared from the periscope lens and he turned and fixed the apparatus on these lights. He centered them in the reticle, increased magnification, and then swept his view toward the ship's prow.

"I see the pennant number: Foxtrot two-three-four," Matias read.

Ledesma flipped pages in his binder, repeated: "F234," and then declared: "*Iron Duke*. That is the frigate that departed *Las Islas Malvinas* right before operations commenced. They must have turned her right around."

Matias leaned into the periscope again and squinted into its eyepiece. "Update: target now at two-six-three degrees. Speed, 11 knots. Bearing, one-seven-zero. Ready tubes two and five. Warm up the weapons."

Ledesma passed the order to the chief-of-the-boat. The chief went to the weapons technician, ordered the fire control system to be updated, and sent orders to the torpedo room.

In the boat's forward-most compartments, two sweating men ducked under racks full of reload torpedoes. They spun valves and checked indicators. One submariner then clicked a switch to talk to the Control Center. He informed the chief that power was flowing to the two telephone pole-sized weapons nestled in the tubes. The chief, in turn, informed the executive officer, who passed confirmation to the captain.

"Power is flowing to tubes two and five. Fire control updates are being transferred," Ledesma reported.

"Flood tubes two and five," Matias ordered.

In the torpedo room, a lever was lowered, and the respective tubes were pumped full of seawater, air was vented, and pressure equalized with that outside the submarine.

"Open outer doors."

Two muzzle doors opened on *San Luis II*'s rounded bow.

Standing behind the Control Room's weapon station, Ledesma confirmed the doors were open.

Matias sighed, breaking the anticipatory silence of the compartment. Then he ordered: "Fire."

The weapons technician pushed a button on his panel.

In the torpedo tubes, a valve slid open and the water ram operated. This plug of high-pressure water pushed both torpedoes from their tubes. Power cables severed, and with safeties now disengaged, both torpedoes activated their onboard kerosene-oxygen turbines. Batteries that powered the torpedoes' guidance systems and warhead fuses came on. Both of *San Luis II*'s weapons began their run. Following their programmed course, the heavy torpedoes turned toward *Iron Duke*'s stern.

The torpedo room technicians immediately went about closing the muzzle doors and draining the tubes of water. When empty and equalized with the submarine's interior, the breeches were reopened and the reloading procedure began.

"Take us down to 500, put us on a parallel course with the target, and drop back 4,000 meters," Matias ordered.

When on electric motors, the submarine was incapable of keeping pace with *Iron Duke*'s current speed, and running the diesels was certain to expose *San Luis II* to counter-attack. Matias told Ledesma that, should the first volley of torpedoes fail to hit, he would then fire a wire-guided weapon and use its high speed to close with and strike the British frigate.

"Very well, sir," Ledesma said as he looked to a light on the weapons console. "Torpedo room reports tubes two and five reloaded." Matias checked his watch.

"Excellent," Matias said, impressed. The captain had sweated the crew in countless drills. Although he heard whispers and grumbling each time, he had reminded his submariners: 'Better to sweat in peacetime than bleed in wartime.' Thousands of yards away, *San Luis II*'s torpedoes began to snake back and forth within the vee of *Iron Duke*'s wake.

The Royal Navy frigate slowed and changed course to take a large wave. As she rode up and over the building-tall upsurge, her stern came up. One torpedo lost track of the frigate's wake and went wide. However, as the stern again displaced water, the second weapon detected its steel and turned toward it. The torpedo struck the bottom of the rolling ship and detonated its 678-pound warhead beneath *Iron Duke*'s main engine room.

The ship shook from stem to stern as it was lifted by the blast and dropped again into the bubble jet created by the explosion.

The keel snapped and superhot gases punched a hole through the hull, cracking and curling its steel. A fireball rose through the ship, venting through the ship's stack and ripping the decking surrounding it. The shockwave from the blast was amplified underwater.

A mile behind and 500 feet below *Iron Duke*, *San Luis II* felt the rumble. A cheer went up, but it was quickly stifled by the officers and the more disciplined. Matias closed his eyes for a moment, knowing that aboard *Iron Duke*, sailors were confronting a hell of twisted metal, smashed machinery, flame, and water.

On *Iron Duke*'s bridge, the shouts of men and the noise of equipment being dragged from repair lockers and hose racks could be heard in nearby areas. Temperature readings from the gas turbines shot up.

"Fire in the main engine room," someone shouted.

The Halon flame-suppression system was started just as the ship's electrical power began to brownout. Generators began to shut down from damage, and the sole remaining one could not handle the demand. It would soon shut down as well. *Iron Duke*'s captain believed he had struck a mine. Certain the Argentinians were incapable of operating this far north, he disagreed with an officer's contention that they had been stalked and attacked by a submarine. Despite this contrary conclusion, the captain ordered that the active sonar be powered up.

"Negative availability, sir," his second-in-command informed him. There was no power for a sonar pulse, let alone weapons.

Iron Duke stopped and bobbed. The warship rolled in the storm and shuddered as she took wave after wave to her broadside. The damaged ship let out an unearthly metallic groan. The sailors did all they could to save her.

A machinist managed to restart the undamaged generator and selectively got power flowing to the fire-fighting pumps and interior lighting. Sailors pounded wooden wedges into bulkhead leaks with mallets. Clothing, mattresses, and pillows were also brought into play to slow down the leaks. Portable eductor pumps began to suck water from the now-flooded main engine and auxiliary machine rooms. The pumps dispatched water overboard from vents and hoses snaking from other hull openings. But despite valiant efforts, *Iron Duke* began to ride lower and lower. After leaning overboard to check the waterline, an officer ran down a darkened passageway.

He passed a burned and bloodied man, naked save for the blanket draped over his shivering shoulders. The officer stopped and, gasping, pointed the way to triage that had been set up in the mess. He then continued on to the bridge, where he went to the officer-of-the-watch and reported: "Sir, we are sinking ourselves."

The reason was firefighters had sprayed tons of water into the ship's skin, and the pumps were being overwhelmed by the accumulating water. This spurred a counter-intuitive order that crackled over the ship's public announcement system: "Cease all firefighting efforts." The captain ordered a damage report.

Inside and out, sailors went about inspections. On the upper deck, the rain, even though lighter now, sizzled on hot metal. Fires flashed, sparked by the hot superstructure, and deck cracks opened everywhere. Smoke billowed from the stricken ship. None of the sailors crawling over *Iron Duke*'s pitching hulk saw the enemy periscope peeking from between waves.

Everyone in *San Luis II*'s Control Room stared at Captain Matias, silently willing him to give the order to launch another torpedo—to deliver the coup de grâce on the British vessel. He scanned their faces.

"*¿Señor?*" Ledesma prodded his captain.

"Take us down to 95 meters; course zero-four-zero. Make turns for five knots," Matias ordered.

Several submariners turned back to their panels, hiding their disgust. Ledesma did not respond at first and simply stared at his captain. Matias had reasoned that the British frigate was combat-ineffective and he refused to slaughter men for no reason. A flame flickered in Matias' eyes. Then he seemed to grow taller and his gaze became stern. Ledesma saw this. Finally, he acknowledged and repeated the order.

The submarine's bow planes tilted downwards. *San Luis II* dived and leaned into her turn. The British survivors had been granted a chance to return home to their families.

4: SHIPWRECK

"Pretend inferiority and encourage his arrogance."—
Sun Tzu

Ominous black thundercaps blanketed the horizon, a wall of flashing, billowing moisture marking the edge of the massive storm. The weather radar display on HMS *Dragon*'s bridge showed a swirling mass of greens, yellows and reds, with patches of blue indicating hailstones. Lightning crackled, fizzled, and ripped across the flashing sky. Rain pattered the ship's windows, and thunder arrived, a rolling boom that trembled the ship. Though gusts still howled outside and the sleek grey hull rose and fell with the churning sea, the tempest moved off. *Dragon* followed a course to skirt the fury's periphery and deliver the warship to her rendezvous with *Iron Duke*.

"Hold onto something," Lieutenant Commander Williams shouted. His voice betrayed the fun of it all. The bridge crew leaned on walls and clutched fixtures as the ship rode up a surge, tipped down again and dove into a deep trough. The ship's prow dug in and heeled before popping up to point skyward again. Someone laughed with glee.

"*Dragon...*" Fryatt whispered her name. He was a proud man.

Dragon, too, was happy. She was in her element and doing that for which she was built. The sharp triangle of her bow buried itself again in the green wash of cold Atlantic water. The ship's bones vibrated. Then the bow came up again, a clawed, snarling, winged, whip-tailed red wyrm painted upon her grey skin. An allusion to figureheads-of-old, the ship's sigil charged through the sea's icy green foaming fingers, warded off evil spirits and sea creatures, and trembled enemies by its ferocity. White spray washed over the wyrm and hissed. Heavy with fuel provisions from her stopover at Ascension Island, *Dragon* steamed south by west toward her rendezvous point.

The revolving spiked ball atop the ship's faceted main tower scanned the airspace for hostiles. Aft of this array and the ship's stack, just forward of the large, flat early warning radar, the communication mast received a flash transmission from Navy Command Headquarters.

"What a mess," Fryatt said to Williams as he read the report. *Iron Duke* had been severely damaged by what was reported as an accidental detonation of her magazine. While she awaited tugs to tow her back to Ascension, *Dragon* was tasked to provide the stricken frigate cover before continuing on to the warzone.

"Detonation?" Williams asked.

"The storm… A missile must have broken loose of its rack and its propellant ignited. You know how unstable ammonium perchlorate is. It probably set off a chain reaction in the magazine," Fryatt posited.

"We are to continue on without a frigate?" Williams added glumly.

"*Argyll* will join us in five days. How long until we get to *Iron Duke*'s position?"

Williams checked their own coordinates, and said: "Within the hour."

By the time *Dragon* came up on *Iron Duke*, the sea-state was down, the water swelling gently into rounded hills. *Iron Duke* rode low by the stern and wallowed in the gentle undulation lapping at her freeboard. A slick surrounded her. Fumes gathered and burned the throats of those on *Dragon*'s decks who leaned against the rails to gawk and offer salutes to any of the frigate's hard-working crew that stole a gaze at the passing destroyer. On the bridge, Captain Fryatt raised his binoculars.

He scanned *Iron Duke*'s hull. He saw some charring, and the pumps busy sending water overboard through multiple openings. Fryatt looked to *Iron Duke*'s mast. The colors flew at half height. His magnified view blurred as it shifted toward the frigate's flight deck where an honor guard went about its solemn duty.

Heads were bowed as a prayer was recited. The heads then raised and salutes were thrown. A body slid from a flag-draped board into the sea. The flag was closed up and encased, and the guard broke up and returned to duties to keep the ship afloat, and to prepare her for a tow.

Accidental detonation. These words stuck uneasily in Fryatt's mind, and the little hairs at the back of his neck stood on end. He surveyed the vast open ocean.

"Power-up the sonar," he ordered. "And get the Merlin up. Cold pattern."

Dragon's MFS-7000 sonar array broadcast a powerful active pulse. Steam bubbles formed around the bow's bulbous protuberance, and a deafening WHOMP emerged. The medium frequency waves propagated through the water for several miles.

In *Dragon*'s Op Room a midshipman studied his sonar screens. He awaited the return of reflected sound waves, awaited the computer's analysis, and looked for a blip that would allow him to yell out: 'Contact.' He was certain that, if anything was submerged within five miles, he would find it. He clicked away at his keyboard and scrutinized the results. *Nothing*, he thought, disappointed.

"Thermocline at 400 feet deep," *Dragon*'s sonarman unenthusiastically told the Operations Director. This meant that warmer water sat atop the colder depths, and thus created an inversion layer where the two varying water masses converged. This layer was impermeable to sound waves, and acted like a false bottom that bounced *Dragon*'s sonar right back at her, providing protection to anything that lurked beneath it. "Otherwise, sir, the scope is clear," the sonarman added.

"Helo's launching," the director responded. The ship's helicopter would use its dipping sonar and sonobuoys to penetrate this layer and expand *Dragon*'s view of the subsurface world.

San Luis II steamed along, doing four knots at 500 feet, some 100 feet beneath the thermocline. The Argentine submariners kept their distance from where they had prosecuted *Iron Duke*, and listened as a new target entered the area. After twenty minutes of analyzing the screw and powerplant noise that the passive sonar had collected, *San Luis II*'s sonar technicians determined they were hearing a *Daring*-class guided-missile destroyer. They designated the surface contact as 'Delta 1.'

"Report," Captain Matias ordered.

"We heard a medium-frequency active sonar. Its transmitter was about eight miles off at one-nine-seven." The sonarman's face shriveled as he listened close. "*Señor*, Delta 1 is slowing."

Matias looked to Ledesma.

"If I was their captain," Ledesma offered, "I would be launching my helicopter."

"Yes, Santiago," Matias confirmed, proud of his protégé.

"Sir, the *D*-class has the Merlin," Ledesma added with a worried look.

Both men had a healthy respect for this particular type of anti-submarine warfare helicopter.

"Take us deeper, Santiago. Two hundred fifty meters."

"*Sí, señor.*"

◊◊◊◊

The Merlin HM2 helicopter emerged from its hangar and traversed onto *Dragon*'s stern flight deck. A haze-grey machine, the Merlin wore a radome on its chin and was configured for anti-submarine warfare with two Stingray lightweight torpedoes and two Mark 11 depth charges slung beneath its parallelogram-shaped fuselage. Emblazoned on the helicopter's side was 'ROYAL NAVY' and a red, white and blue roundel.

The Flight Deck Officer saluted to the helicopter's pilot, indicating the flight deck chief had the wheel chocks in place and there was no sign of foreign objects that the Merlin's engines or rotors could suck in. The Merlin's pilot—Lieutenant Seamus McLaughlin from Enniskillen, Northern Ireland—loved to fly. Beneath his flight helmet, Seamus the pilot had fire red hair and a 'full set'—Royal Navy-speak for a beard and mustache. Seamus moved a control panel lever, and the helicopter's five main rotor blades unfolded from their ship-stowed position and locked in place. With a nod from the Merlin's secondary pilot, Seamus started the helicopter's three turboshaft engines. The engines coughed black smoke as they ignited and then whined as they spun up. Seamus performed his pre-departure radio checks.

"Draig, Kingfisher 21, radio check, over," Seamus said into his headset. Due to his thick Irish accent, he had learned to speak slowly and clearly when using the radio.

"Kingfisher two-one, Draig, loud and clear, over," *Dragon*'s air traffic controller responded.

The helicopter pilots went through pre-flight checklists in the front of the machine, and in its rear cabin, the Merlin's observer and aircrewman went about their own tasks. The observer was Ordinary Seaman Rodi Dando whom hailed from Dockyard on the Spanish Point of Bermuda and was the descendant of an African privateer. Also operating in the rear cabin was Merlin's aircrewman, Leading Seaman John Mcelaney.

Aircrewman John Mcelaney was a wide-shouldered lad from Liverpool. He had grown up in New Brighton on the Wirral Peninsula where sandy beaches overlooked the River Mersey and the Irish Sea. Working these waterways,

John had hauled in crab traps and fishing nets for his father and uncle, a job that built his upper-body strength and log-like arms. When the waters had become overfished and the ill-maintained family boats leaked more than floated, John sought to see more of the world. With college funds scant, it was a Royal Marine recruiter who had bought him a pint in the pub and seduced him with tales of adventure and travel. John signed on the dotted line. He awoke to a headache, sour stomach and a lecture from his mum and dad, but he soon embarked to Commando Training Centre Royal Marines in Lympstone, Devon. Thirty-two weeks of hell followed.

At Lympstone, John learned combat skills—to march and look after his kit and weapons—and he earned the vaunted green beret. Fit and as sharp as a sword, John volunteered for transfer, and after grading at an air force base, he was sent on to anti-submarine training. Ten weeks at 824 Naval Air Squadron's Basic Acoustic Course followed.

John seemed to have an innate talent for the fine art of sonar and sensor operation, and this was recognized and nurtured by instructors. High marks and performance reports drove advancement to an operational conversion unit.

At the OCU, John met the love of his life—the Merlin HM2—and worked alongside a pair of pilots and an observer. He had learned the art of active and passive anti-submarine warfare, as well as search and prosecution techniques. It was not long afterward that he was honored with assignment to HMS *Dragon*.

John powered-up and then checked the helicopter's various defensive and offensive systems, including chaff, flares, and the FLASH dipping sonar. The FLASH— Folding Light Acoustic System for Helicopters—could lower by cable a tube-shaped low-frequency sonar transducer down to 700 meters beneath the sea.

The Merlin's cockpit screens flashed and became populated with brightly-colored data as the computer examined the helicopter thousands of times per second and delivered the diagnoses to its human operators. With all indicators in the green, Seamus engaged the rotors and started them spinning.

"Sir," John's voice crackled on the intercom, "All systems are go."

With a "Ready," from his secondary, Seamus clicked the transmitter:

"Kingfisher 21, ready for departure."

Clearance was received and blade revolutions came up to take-off power. The Flight Deck Chief indicated chocks were out and that no tie-downs were in use. Then the Flight Deck Officer saluted and, slowly flapping his arms, marshaled the Merlin off the deck. Seamus raised the collective. The main rotor tilted and bit into the air, where vortices formed at its shovel blade-shaped tips. The Merlin rose over *Dragon*'s stern.

The helicopter hovered over the flight deck and swiveled into the relative wind. It then flew sideways to a hover position alongside the ship. Clear of deck hazards— the hangar, the masts, and radar arrays—the Merlin began a straight climb and fell back as *Dragon* continued onward at seven knots. Holding a hover at 300 feet, Seamus surveyed the instruments, switched to the high-frequency radio, and confirmed their machine was healthy and under positive control. He requested permission to depart the pattern.

"Kingfisher two-one, Draig, roger, commence your turn on course," the ship's air traffic control responded.

Seamus pushed his boot against a pedal and pointed the Merlin's nose in the desired direction, nudging the cyclic. The big helicopter leaned forward and headed away from the churned, light-blue wake of the destroyer. In the distance, where the last of the rain darkened the horizon line, a cloud discharged and sent a forked bolt snaking from the sea to high in the sky. Seamus started down the first leg of his pattern. In the rear cabin, John prepared to lower the dipping sonar while the observer, Rodi, peered out the window.

Dragon circled *Iron Duke* in a mile-wide circle. Far on the horizon, the smoke trail of the Royal Navy tugboat became visible.

The tug was *Capable*, an *Adept*-class large harbor tug based in Gibraltar. *Dragon* had her on radar, and Lieutenant-Commander Williams was talking to her by radio. As a harbor tug not ideal for the mission of getting *Iron Duke* to safe waters—especially all by her lonesome—*Capable* had adequate power. If only the weather held, she also had the seaworthiness to depart the near-shore environment for the open sea. If all went well, *Capable* would pull *Iron Duke* back to Ascension for temporary repairs, freeing *Dragon* to race to the Falklands. It would be hours until *Capable* could arrive on-scene, however. Several long, dangerous hours. Captain Fryatt paced the bridge.

Fryatt felt the gentle roll of the ship in his ears and made a picture of the battlespace in his mind's eye: *Iron Duke* was at the center as *Dragon* swept around her; the Merlin was off doing its task, dropping sonobuoys and listening to the ocean, making sure no submarines could sneak in to threaten either vessel. Then Fryatt's mind's eye dove beneath the waves. He pictured the thermocline that shrouded the deeps, and he saw what he knew of the bottom at this part of the Atlantic: mud flats and rocky foothills that climbed to become the craggy peaks of the Mid-Atlantic

Ridge, Earth's longest mountain range, the 'spine of the world.'

5: CAT AND MOUSE

"*When the mouse laughs at the cat, there's a hole nearby.*"—Nigerian proverb

They called him '*Raton*.' Not, mind you, because of any inherent trait, nor for any physical resemblance to the little furry, whisker-twitching mammal. For Raton's face was flat, almost indented, and lacked the rat's snout-like structure. Though his first name was Gaston—a convenient and almost lyrical rhyme with his nickname—Corporal Second Class Bersa earned his moniker by the style of life he lived aboard *San Luis II*.

Gaston Bersa came from Salta, a small farming town in the Lerma valley of Argentina's northwest. His family farm would be desert dry if not for the water delivered by canal and pipe from the snow-capped mountains that towered above it. With this precious moisture, lemons and oranges grew where only dust devils and brown brush should flourish. Days of hard work were broken by reading in the shade, moments where he would take out his tattered Cuban-translated copy of Hemingway's 'The Old Man and the Sea,' digesting it for the hundredth time and reciting each word as if by memory. And dreaming of the blue open sea and the freedom it imparted.

A sustained drought had come, causing the government to divert water to the thirsty cities. Soon the groves browned and died and Gaston's father had taken to doing odd construction and repair jobs in town, leaving him to watch his small sister and his broken-down mother. One day the pages of his novel had finally fallen out and been taken by the wind. They scattered over the bones of the citrus trees. That day, Gaston had dropped his shovel and walked the six miles to town. He did not even know why he made the trek, and he could not argue with the sensation of being drawn that way. Once among the town's squat buildings and dust-choked streets, he trudged past out-of-work farm hands and right into a government office.

Gaston had meant to yell and curse at whoever was there. He would lecture the bureaucrats on water and farms and how crops were more important than keeping the fountains going in Buenos Aires. Before he began his tirade, however, he became transfixed by a picture of a navy ship that rode up a sea-swell. The local recruiter saw the look in Gaston's eye and smiled.

"*¿Hermosa, no?*" he asked the entranced youth.

"Yes. *Very* beautiful."

"There is nothing like being aboard ship, sailing the seas and doing so for your country." The recruiter set the hook, knowing full well it was submariners the navy was currently in need of.

"Yes," Gaston repeated.

His signature and acceptance of a small cash bonus meant that Gaston Bersa now belonged to *Comando de la Fuerza de Submarinos*—the submarine branch of the Argentine Navy.

That night was the last time Gaston had seen his mother and father, or the stars that hung above the Lerma valley. Almost two years since had passed in rigorous basic and submarine training, and then *San Luis II* became Gaston's new home.

Like everyone aboard *Numero Dos*, Raton was condemned to near-darkness and hot, stuffy breaths. However, unlike the others, Raton's duties were especially rodential, the nature of which imparted his new nickname.

Chosen for his diminutive stature, wiry frame, and seeming immunity to claustrophobia, Raton spent most of his time at the bottom of *San Luis II*'s pressure hull where he lay upon his belly and slid a rail-borne sled over the submarine's two battery banks.

San Luis II's battery deck entailed a thicket of power cables, leads, and ventilation tubes that grew from row-after-row of foot locker-sized two-ton battery cells. It stank of battery acid, diesel, and salt. It was an underworld where the footfalls of fellow crewmates reverberated through the low ceiling. This was Raton's nest. Despite the drawbacks, it was a place of privacy in a big unprivate, a place where technical knowledge made him ruler. He scurried along on his sled maintaining his batteries.

Raton checked each for corrosion, repaired ventilation nipples, and topped the cells off with distilled water. In this dim loneliness hid Raton's thoughts, his hummed folksongs, and largely unnoticed by the boat's officers, intermittent naps. With a flashlight headband to see his work, and with a hearty yawn, Raton checked the compartment's hydrogen meter.

The meter indicated that the odorless, tasteless, and highly flammable gas—produced when the water portion of the battery was converted during charging—remained within safe limits. Raton checked a small flow meter on a cell's ventilation duct header. The number indicated that the ventilators were doing their job of shunting the hydrogen to holding tanks, to be blown overboard. Before Raton wiggled and tightened an inter-cell connector wire, he checked the voltmeter and muttered a prayer.

He did this whenever he touched anything down here. Even though he knew his job inside out, everything around him was built by what he called 'Vodka-infused Russian dockworkers,' and was really just updated Cold War technology. It did not help his nerves or superstitions that a man was killed on the battery deck during the boat's shakedown cruise.

San Luis II had been built for the Indian Navy. Named *Varuna* for the Hindu God of the Ocean, a contract spat between Moscow and New Dehli meant the submarine was instead counter-traded with Buenos Aires for copper. She was then renamed and, like all Argentine submarines, received the name of an Argentine province that began with an 'S,' and thus became the second Argentine submarine named *San Luis*. The first *San Luis* had performed a central role in commando actions during the 1982 conflict over *Las Islas Malvinas*. When *Numero Dos* had sailed on its shakedown cruise, a cell's vent valve failed and burst. Covered with acid and burned by heat, Raton's predecessor had died down here on the battery deck.

Raton had seen him once, he would swear. It was a ghostly head that stared back at him and smiled. So, Raton was always thankful when his job did not kill him. As he pulled his hand away from the battery, he knew that God, for now, had decided to keep him alive.

"*Amén*," Raton mumbled. He grabbed at handholds and slid the sled a few more feet to check a cable junction. Like his fellow submariners, Raton had heard the reverberation of the active sonar ping, and felt it vibrate through his prone body. He ignored such things, however, and trusted in his captain and crewmates to keep him alive, just as they all relied on him to keep *San Luis II*'s air blowing, motor running, and keep the lights on. Whenever Raton's mind turned to darker doubts, he would slide along on his sled and find something else to check or repair. When the next sonar ping—higher in frequency this time— echoed through *San Luis II*'s bilges, Raton paused and suddenly felt the tight confines and helpless vulnerability of his situation. As much as he loved the sea, down here beneath it, the sea had become his enemy. He knew its embrace would not be warm and gentle, but cold and hard.

In *San Luis II*'s Control Room, Ledesma reported to Matias: "Dipping sonar at two-three-six. Range: five miles." Another ping and everyone cringed. "It's the helicopter, sir...The Merlin."

The Merlin's rotor chopped at the air. The 30,000-pound machine hovered and performed a delicate balancing act of physics and thrust. The rotor wash sent white-capped waves off in a wide circle, while a steel cable unwound from beneath the Merlin's fuselage. The FLASH dipping sonar splashed through the surface and continued downward into the depths. In the Merlin's computer-filled cabin, John turned his dial to stop its descent. He hit a red button.

At 100 feet beneath the surface, the FLASH sent out a high-frequency pulse. Then it listened for a return. John announced what everyone already knew: "Significant layer at 410 feet." He adjusted a dial to unreel more cable, dipping the FLASH beneath the thermocline.

"Cable now at 500 feet. Hammer."

Another ping. The sound wave traveled in all directions, reaching for the bottom of the Atlantic. As the computer analyzed returns, an image began filling the display in the helicopter's rear cabin. It showed the undulating sea bottom, the false 'ceiling' of the thermocline, a clustered school of fish and…an ovoid shadow. A red light flashed above the screen.

"Submerged contact," John announced. "Depth: 600 feet. Bearing: zero-six-zero. Range: five miles. Designate 'Possub.'" A possible submarine. The FLASH was reeled in so the Merlin could move again.

As contact data was relayed to *Dragon*'s Action Information Center, Seamus tipped the helicopter's nose down and began a sprint toward the contact's coordinates. Captain Fryatt would place *Dragon* between the contact and *Iron Duke*, but the Merlin's mission was to localize and attack any target. The Merlin continued its charge, sprinting at just over 180 miles-per-hour. It covered several miles in just minutes. Rodi leaned his head into the cabin window and raised his binoculars.

"A lot of water," Rodi said with his Bermudian lilt.

The grey shapes of *Dragon* and *Iron Duke* were now far on the horizon. A high-pressure front had pushed the storm away, drying and heating the air and creating a shimmering haze where sea met sky. It made the grey outline of the warships hard to see. Furthermore, *Dragon*'s rather significant but white superstructure blended it into the bright sky. In the Merlin, John alerted Seamus of their proximity to their first drop.

The first sonar buoy shot free of the aircraft's fuselage. Pushed from its tube by high-pressure air, the cylindrical sensor splashed in and then bobbed at the surface. It deployed its whip antenna and unfolded its transducers. The buoy found a global positioning satellite and logged its location, and then made contact with the Merlin's computer. The first of many to be deployed in a diamond-shaped pattern, this sonobuoy was of the bathythermograph type, designed to ascertain local density, salinity and temperature conditions. The next sonobuoys the Merlin deployed would be DIFAR and HIDAR types. The DIFARs would provide direction to any particular producer of sound, and the HIFARs would instantaneously provide the target's range. The Merlin sprinted and dropped, sprinted and dropped, repeating this process, surrounding the original contact with listening devices. When the pattern was complete, Seamus shoved his stick over.

The Merlin screamed toward the center of the pattern, where the FLASH had first discovered the anomalous contact among the sonar returns from the rocky bottom, the swimming fish, and haunting whale songs. The Merlin raised its nose to rapidly shed airspeed until it virtually stood still, Seamus leveling his aircraft and nursing the hover. He balanced the collective and cyclic sticks and engine power as well, until he became in tune with every breeze and pull of gravity, keeping his machine steady and floating in place above the sparkling ocean. When he felt ready, he gave clearance to the cabin crew. From the helicopters belly, the dipping sonar descended.

The FLASH unreeled again and penetrated the water's surface, falling to breach that problematic thermocline. It would peek beneath this layer to verify and firm up data on the previous contact. As the FLASH did its job, John

monitored the sonobuoys that listened for any possible

transitory signals. Kingfisher 21—*Dragon*'s Merlin—had

cast its net wide. Now, it began to cinch it and haul it in.

The passive array that ran the length of *San Luis II*'s

hull heard the thump-thump-thump of an approaching

helicopter, and then the splashes of sonobuoys.

Indoctrinated and trained by Argentines, each submariner

had nonetheless studied and held a secret admiration for

their British enemy. After all, the *británicos* had overcome

the German U-boat threat by developing tactics and

technology that had turned the table on the greatest

underwater mariners humankind had ever known. They then

had joined the Americans in corralling the Soviet threat,

whose machines and men threatened to rule the world. This

secret admiration of the British by the Argentines also

indicated an unconscious fear, and fear always meant hesitation. As much as it was Captain Matias' job to keep his boat from going to the bottom, it was also his job to inspire the crew to believe they were better than those British, who seemed to think they had a God-given right to dominate affairs. As much as Captain Matias believed *Las Islas Malvinas* were not worth the risk, he would fight for his flag, and for those placed under his command. His thoughts were interrupted by a sound from outside.

Captain Matias knew that his submarine created hydrodynamic noise resulting from the flow of water over its hull. Any protrusions and orifices such as bollards and free-flood holes, accentuated this noise. Even though the Russian builders had tried their best to minimize such sources, the propeller remained an insurmountable acoustic problem for any submarine.

When on batteries, diesel-electric boats like *San Luis II* enjoyed advantages over their atom-smashing counterparts, because there were no unbalanced turbine gears, blades and cooling pumps to make a racket and reveal their position. However, like their nuclear cousins, diesel-electrics had to transfer propulsive power from an engine to the water, making the propeller the acoustic weak link in the whole nearly silent system. In *San Luis II*'s case, it was a single giant six-bladed prop that did the job.

At the tips of this carefully-machined wonder, vortex cavitation took place, whereby air bubbles formed and collapsed under sea pressure, producing a hissing sound that carried for miles underwater. This noise travelled horizontally from the propeller, increased with the momentum of the blades, and became most pronounced at high speed, especially during acceleration and maneuvers. At lower speeds, the natural frequency of the blades produced a characteristic 'beat' that an enemy could use to identify the specific class of his adversary. Sometimes, unique acoustic 'fingerprints' would even allow a skilled sonarman to identify a submarine by name. Such noise was the very clue Captain Matias sought to deprive his enemy, the very reason he had ordered: 'All stop.' Despite his efforts to silence *San Luis II*, there remained the issue of her physicality. She was, after all, a steel hole in the water, and despite precautions against detection by passive systems, active sonar, such as that carried by the enemy helicopter, constituted another matter altogether.

"Get us closer to the bottom, Santiago," Matias ordered. The captain hoped the seamount off to starboard would screen his boat and spoil any acoustic reflection that would allow the British aircrew to discern the hull of *San Luis II* from among the boulders, cliffs, and peaks of the Mid-Atlantic Ridge. Already near their recommended maximum depth, Ledesma shot the captain a concerned

glance. "Down," Matias reiterated.

Ledesma hesitated for a moment, and Matias waved a

hand at him that said, 'Get on with it.'

"*Muy bien señor*," Ledesma finally acknowledged,

and ordered negative buoyancy. Vents on the outer hull

were opened, and more seawater flowed into *San Luis II*'s

main ballast tanks. Already stationary, the boat dropped

straight down into the pitch black deep. The men in the

Control Room watched the depth gauge needle move from

the yellow zone, into the red. The steel hull protested with

clicks, groans, and tortured snaps. Ledesma swallowed hard

and began to read off the depth: "Three hundred twenty;

330; 340…" The boat protested with a loud bang.

The ocean tested *San Luis II*. It wanted in, and it

searched for the path of least resistance. Thousands of

pounds pressed on the submarine. Another bang, and

everyone looked to Captain Matias. He looked up the main ladder at the Control Room hatch. BANG. The thinner steel of the submarine's sail had flexed under extreme pressure and deformed, stretching between its latticed framework.

"Deeper," the captain ordered.

San Luis II let out a prolonged noise like the song of a melancholy whale. One submariner began to breathe heavily, and then he whimpered.

"*Tomalo con soda*," Ledesma calmed the neophyte submariner with an Argentine expression. Then he turned to Matias. "*Señor, estamos a 360 metros.*" Then came an unholy creak from *San Luis II*. "I don't think she can stand much more," Ledesma pleaded.

"*Bien*, Santiago," Matias conceded, "Hold us here."

"Neutral buoyancy," Ledesma said, pointing at the vent levers. "Hold your depth at 380 meters."

The boat quieted as the depth gauge steadied and stopped, just a few hash marks short of '400,' the highest number the dial showed. Someone sighed with relief, followed by a moment of silence, of calm. Then suddenly, a water pipe running along the top of the Control Center whined and burst.

Water sprayed from a valve and ran along the pipe, raining down.

"Damage control," Ledesma yelled.

The valve shot off and bounced twice. The deck plate it hit rang fantastically loud. The metal wheel wobbled for a moment and then stopped. Everyone in the Control Room looked at it, hated it, and knew what it had done.

One sailor immediately took a wrench to the valve and instantly became soaked by the leak, yet he tightened the connection. The water slowed, but still it cascaded down a panel.

Sparks flashed and the panel's display lights extinguished. However, back-up analog displays confirmed the tank vents had in fact closed. Valves were opened and closed along the pipe in order to isolate the leak. Everyone looked to the curved ceiling. They all wondered if the enemy had heard the commotion.

"*Señor*, the leak has been isolated," Ledesma whispered.

"Very well," Captain Matias acknowledged.

PING.

"Sir, active--"

PING.

"Yes, Santiago," Matias put his hand on his friend's shoulder, "I hear it."

6: ABRAZO

"Let me embrace thee, sour adversity, for wise men say it is the wisest course."—William Shakespeare

Kingfisher 21 hovered. The Merlin's dipping sonar dangled in the water, fishing for anything that happened to be biting. Among the miles-wide sonobuoy field *Dragon*'s helicopter had sown, one passive type—buoy 'Papa Three'—had registered an anomalous sound. It transmitted to the helicopter the contact's general depth, heading, and range. Kingfisher 21, in turn, bounced the data back to *Dragon*.

In the Op Room's cool darkness, *Dragon*'s anti-submarine warfare officer adjusted his flash hood and gloves and surveyed his screen. It showed the GPS plot of each sonobuoy, and represented by a green 'H,' the radar position of the helicopter.

The Merlin had raced to sonobuoy Papa Three's position and hurriedly lowered its dipping sonar below the thermocline. John fired off an active ping. The sound waves moved through the liquid medium, where they bounced off shoals of fish, off rock, and off sand, and off anything else in the oceanic water column. Then the sound waves boomeranged and returned to, and were collected by, the FLASH's cylindrical transmitter/receiver. Tied into the buoys, the computers in the Merlin's rear cabin analyzed the data and presented it on a monochrome screen.

An object differing from the contours of the sea bottom immediately caught John's highly trained eye. John tapped the display's glass in recognition.

"What have we here?" he mumbled to himself, and then pushed the transmit button for his headset. "Draig TACCO, this is Kingfisher 21. PROBSUB, PROBSUB," John reported to *Dragon*'s tactical coordinator. He then switched from the radio to the intercom. "Dropping smoke," he told the Merlin's pilot.

A small cartridge was fired from the helicopter's wheel-wells that splashed in, stained the water a glowing green, and sent up a plume of red smoke. This marker would help Seamus maintain position over the contact, and also mark the contact position for the destroyer. On the horizon, *Dragon* turned.

Captain Fryatt peered through binoculars. He found the red smoke cloud, glanced at the compass, and ordered a heading: "Make your course two-five-five." It was the captain's intent to keep the destroyer's sharp bow and towering superstructure between *Iron Duke* and 'Master 1,' the tactical coordinator's designation for the probable submerged submarine.

"Ahead full," Fryatt ordered. *Dragon*'s two Rolls-Royce gas turbines revved up and drove the ship's electric motors. The bow rose, and *Dragon*'s sleek, grey hull planed, churning the dark water as white as milk. *Dragon* became an 8,000 ton speedboat. A minute later, 27,000 shaft horsepower had shot the destroyer to over 30 knots. She turned to her new heading, leaned in, and threw spray up in a great fan. Fryatt intended, once at the contact coordinate, to use *Dragon*'s powerful bow sonar to localize Master 1. *Dragon* drove a wind before her, and as if pushed by it, the Merlin banked off.

The Merlin was guided by *Dragon*'s Op Room to her next hunting position. The helicopter dropped its nose and raced off, to dip its sonar again and add a vertex angle to the triangulation of the contact.

The sound of the dropped valve wheel bounced its way down to the confines of Raton's domain. The repeating clang reverberated through the battery deck and when the echoes subsided, Raton looked to the submarine's cold inner steel hull. Despite its thickness and strength, the hull was an ideal transmitter of sound.

This was the reason internal machinery was isolated from the boat's skin wherever possible, Raton pondered as he fingered a rubber cylinder that supported his own sled's track. He felt the track's metal and recognized the vibration from *San Luis II*'s diesels.

They, too, were dampened, mounted on big rubber rafts that kept their reverberations from transmitting to *San Luis II*'s casing. These efforts, however, could be undone by a hatch closed too hard, a fallen tool, or in this case, a dropped wheel valve. All of these could provide potentially lethal results. *That piece of iron shit*, Raton postulated. *It was forged in some old Murmansk furnace. The noise it made was surely heard by the clams and fish and those maldito británicos.* Raton caught his breath and held the air in his lungs as he heard a trickle of water.

The sound was different from that created by the flow of water around *San Luis II*'s hull, and different from the bubbles of trapped air that occasionally escaped the casing's free-flood areas. The sound, Raton realized, had come from inside.

The water that had escaped the Control Room pipe valve had then found its way down the periscope well. Tugged by gravity, it sought the most direct path possible to the lowest point in the boat, the bilge. However, between the Control Room and bilge was the battery deck where, craning his neck, Raton saw the first signs of the water.

Held fast by surface tension, the water clung to the steel roof and squirmed and squiggled along in a streamer that split and merged again. Raton watched and kept pace. He scooted his sled along the compartment rails, his belly just over the tangle of leads and wire that grew from the battery cells. The water ran into a small protuberance where, no longer able to defy gravity, it stretched into a long drop over an electrical shunt and disconnect switch. Raton hurried to put his gloved hand on the switch. He watched the drop elongate.

The liquid orb reflected the lights and machinery of the confined space. Raton saw himself there, too, a stretched face with wide eyes and a sweat-covered brow. He cursed the water. Then he thought of the cool summer thunderstorms that visited his farm in Salta, where the rains would break the humidity and drench the croplands. Before they called him 'Raton,' he was Gaston Bersa, a simple farmer, a man who stood among the rows of citrus trees and let the downpour wash away the day's dirt and sweat.

Raton had fallen in love with the sea at first. It had helped him escape the workaday life, and offered him a perfumed, salty-sweet smell and a vast openness he had never before experienced. But soon he came to consider the whole other world, beneath the undulating plane of the sea's surface.

Submarine school imparted a healthy fear of, and respect for, that domain. High-pressure water had sprayed Raton and his classmates, filling the training compartment fast. He then learned that the ocean was the enemy, something to be resisted and fought. When mechanical aptitude and a slight frame had gotten him assigned to the battery deck, he quickly learned that, should saltwater contact the electrolyte within the imperfectly sealed battery cells, a plume of lethal chlorine gas would flood the compartment, and potentially the entire submarine. Raton snapped the disconnect switch over, and isolated a block of batteries.

The water seemed to fall all at once, a brief rain that splattered across the square tops of the battery cells. *I love my job*, Raton thought ironically. He began to hum; his usual remedy for doubt or fear. Then his tight little world was shattered by another sonar ping. This one was lower in frequency and clearly more powerful, for it shook the very skin of *San Luis II*.

◊◊◊◊

"Active sonar…and propeller noises," *San Luis II*'s sonar technician announced. "Twin screws," he added. "It is Delta 1, sir. The destroyer. She has turned in our direction, and is closing fast." 'Destroyer.' The word bore so much weight to submariners. Throughout history, such ships were both respected and cursed by those that lurked and sneaked about beneath the sea. Captain Matias looked to Ledesma, who rolled his eyes, a gesture that communicated much.

"Sir, airborne contact," the sonar technician said. With the thermocline breaking up, *San Luis II*'s sonar could now discern the high rpm turbine and thumping rotors of the hovering Merlin. "Designate: 'Hotel 1.'"

The Merlin—that vexatious helicopter that seemed to appear and disappear to aggravate the very captain who had kept them alive so far—now had a designation, a neat packet to contain the venom they felt for this contraption. Matias looked at the clock. *1930. It's getting dark top-side.* Then the Control Room lights flickered.

"Report," he ordered.

Ledesma looked to the Control Room's engineering panel and the battery read-outs, and then his gaze shifted to the electrician's mate whose job it was to monitor the boat's systems. Grasping for an answer, the electrician's mate threw switches, pushed buttons, and read gauges.

"Sir, voltage drop," he reported. "I show a manual tripping of 'primary disconnect one.' Available power now down to 22 percent."

Ledesma went to the growler, lifted the receiver, and selected the battery deck. After he made inquiries, Ledesma hung up and turned to the captain.

"Battery deck reports bank two isolated due to water. Corporal Bersa is trying to get another eight percent with cable bridging."

"Goddamn it." Matias knew that, with battery reserves so low, he would soon need to run the diesels, and the diesels needed air.

"Captain, we must decrease our depth," Ledesma beseeched. Just then, in seeming support of his recommendation, begging for relief from the black crush, *San Luis II* let out a shudder and a prolonged groan.

"Very well," Matias added with the calm of someone with nothing to lose. *If I am forced to the surface*, the captain thought, *I will put my boot right up their ass*. Although Matias had already made up his mind on a course of action, he asked Ledesma for advice nonetheless: "Options?"

"Well, sir, there are not many. Just one really," Ledesma raised his eyebrows into a black arch. Matias nodded.

"*Maldito británicos*," someone mumbled. They had eavesdropped on the officer's conversation—not hard inside a steel pipe that amplified mere whispers and bounced them in all directions. Matias's bowed head lifted. He strolled the compartment and surveyed the men under his command. He could have asked, 'Who said this? Who was undisciplined enough to offer such a statement?' Though, in this case, he would not make an example for the sake of discipline. Why? Fatigue mainly, and because Captain Matias agreed with the comment. *Yes, damn the British.*

"*Señor*," Ledesma sought his captain's attention once again.

"*¿Si, Santiago?*"

"Captain, we must attack."

Captain Matias studied his executive officer, liking what he heard, and the look of determination in his subordinate's eyes.

"What is the moon like this evening?" the captain inquired.

Ledesma consulted a table.

"Waning crescent."

Good, Matias thought and nodded, *the light of the moon will not be on their side.* Matias closed his eyes and pictured the silvery surface. He longed for a lungful of fresh, salt-laden sea air. He thought of submariners of old who used to bring their boat to the surface, pop the hatch, and climb out onto the conning tower to line up an attack as sea spray drenched their stink away, and fresh breezes carried away their cares.

Yes, he thought, *damn the British, and damn it all to hell.* After all, anything was better than hiding down here in the blackness.

"Okay, my darling," Matias whispered as he stroked the nearest piece of the submarine's metal that his shaking hand could find. Then his voice boomed: "Ten degrees rise on the bow."

"Yes, my captain."

"Load tubes one and six with Klubs, and put Squalls in two and five," Matias had ordered anti-ship cruise missiles and rocket-propelled torpedoes.

Ledesma grinned.

"Keep '53s' in three and four," Matias added, wanting the wake-homing torpedoes available as well.

"Aye, sir." Ledesma was re-energized by the new order, and it was soon repeated and transmitted to the bow compartment.

Technicians in the weapons room scurried about as their supervisor shouted instructions. In a well-practiced dance, six men unloaded wake-homing torpedoes from four tubes, winched them back onto storage racks, and then loaded the encapsulated missiles and cone-shaped rocket-propelled torpedoes. Their supervisor smiled at his panting men, thankful for the frequent skill-sharpening drills. He cranked the growler.

"Sir," Ledesma said as he put down the growler in the Control Center. "Bow compartment reports all tubes loaded and ready in all respects."

"Excellent," Captain Matias looked at his watch. "Record time."

The submarine seemed excited by the new action. With nose pointed toward the waves, *San Luis II* rose fast, like a swimmer who had gone too deep for too long and felt that insatiable urge to suck air again.

"Mind your rise," Matias said, and watched as the bow angle was checked and adjusted. The indicator bubble moved from 12 degrees to the proper 10 he had ordered. Creaks, bubbling, and the sound of rushing water sounded, as though a tap had been opened.

"Delta 1 and Hotel 1 continue to close," the sonar technician's raspy voice added to the sounds.

◊◊◊◊

Captain Fryatt grabbed one of the bridge handholds
that the genius engineers at BAE Systems had had the
foresight to install. He was amazed that someone seated at a
cubicle far from the fury of the Atlantic could look beyond
their desk, beyond the flatscreen that displayed the ship's
three-dimensional design, and transpose themselves into the
reality of a fighting ship at sea. Fryatt peered out through
the spray-soaked bridge window. The colorful sunset made
it difficult to see the marker smoke dropped by the Merlin.
Then he spotted the ribbon that rose from the water.

Fryatt ordered a slight course correction, "Come three
degrees to port." When he was happy with the bow's
alignment, he said: "Steady as she goes." Captain Fryatt
smiled. He did not need radar or sonar, nor any of the
glowing, digital readouts his amazing ship offered. *'I must
go down to the seas again, to the vagrant gypsy life.'* The

quote was displaced by an electronic beeping and his first officer's report:

"Sonar reports Master 1 is at zero-nine-five. Depth: 330 meters and rising. Bearing: zero-one-eight. She is making turns for eight knots."

"Clear Kingfisher to prosecute."

"Aye, sir," Williams turned and nodded. The simple gesture would forward authorization to the Merlin to attack the contact.

"Bow array. Hammer," Fryatt added. The sonar in *Dragon*'s bulbous bow powered-up to send sound waves into the deep.

WHOMP.

San Luis II's metal hull shook as the sound waves hit her. Only the enemy destroyer could put such power behind its sensor.

"Get us to missile launch depth quickly. They will be shitting all over us in a second," Ledesma barked to the Control Center personnel.

"Bow up 20," the chief said as he rested his hand on the planesman's shoulder. *San Luis II* pitched up. The floor of the submarine's Control Center became a steep hill. Those standing braced themselves, while those seated secured seatbelts. The floor tilted toward starboard. "Watch your trim, damn it; watch your trim." the chief barked. The helmsman and planesman used all their ability and skill to arrive at the missile firing depth smartly.

Just forward of *San Luis II*'s sail, the maneuvering planes articulated to steady the speeding hull as water was pumped into a port-side tank. *San Luis II*'s roll leveled out.

Captain Matias smiled, confident that *San Luis II* was in good hands. He said: "Make tubes three and four ready in all respects, including opening outer doors."

Ledesma repeated the orders, and seconds later, reported they had been carried out.

"Very well. Firing point procedures, tubes three and four, surface target: Delta 1. Fire."

San Luis II shuddered as the two heavy wake-homing torpedoes shot from her hull.

"Torpedoes away, tubes three and four," Ledesma said with a smile. "My depth is 180 meters headed for 30."

"Close outer doors and reload tubes three and four with '53s. Slow ascent at 100 meters and open outer doors, tubes one, two, five, and six. At 30 meters, snap shot those tubes. Start with two and five, then one and six, all targeting Delta 1."

"Aye, sir," Ledesma acknowledged with a clenched jaw, and precisely repeated the complex orders to subordinates. "Sir, bow compartment reports tubes three and four reloaded and ready in all respects.

Matias nodded. Silence hung in the Control Room, and tension among the crew was as heavy as the recirculated air.

"Splashes and high-pitch screw; torpedo in the water," the sonar supervisor announced. "Range: 1,000 yards; bearing and course changing rapidly," the young man's voice cracked.

"Hotel 1," Ledesma mumbled. The Merlin had dropped one of its Stingray lightweight homing torpedoes, now descending in a helical pattern.

"Torpedo is active and searching." The Stingray's active sonar had energized, and was looking for something to kill.

"Rig boat for depth charges. Launch noisemaker," Matias barked, his orders now clipped as the stress of the encounter increased. Each of *San Luis II*'s compartments prepared for damage control. The torpedo room fed a cylindrical noisemaker into tube seven, a small vertical ejector that protruded from the compartment's ceiling. The noisemaker contained chemicals that reacted with salt water and thus effervesced, creating an ensonified area that would appear on enemy sonar.

"*Señor*, bow compartment reports 'noisemaker is away,'" Ledesma informed the captain. Reading Matias' mind, he added: "My depth is 70 meters headed for 30. Our torpedoes are bearing: zero-nine-seven. Course: zero-one-five degrees. Both are running straight and normal." He glanced at the depth gauge. "We're at 50 meters."

"Slow the ascent, trim the boat, and open outer doors, tubes one, two, five, and six," Matias was squinting and focused. The captain grabbed ceiling pipes and wireways to steady himself as he walked toward the fire control panel. As *San Luis II* came shallow, the men could hear the rhythmic whooshing of *Dragon*'s propellers through the hull. Down in the battery deck, Raton likened the noise to that of cicadae on a hot summer's night.

Ledesma spun around to inform Matias, "Outer doors open. We're at 30 meters,"

Matias took a deep breath and gave the order: "Firing point procedures on Delta 1. Snapshot, tubes one, two, five, and six."

After a loud hiss of air, San *Luis II* shimmied for several seconds.

"Weapons are away," Ledesma announced.

"Close outer doors, all tubes. Crash dive. Make your depth 300 meters. Reload tubes one, two, five, and six with '53s."

"Crash dive. Crash dive," Ledesma yelled. A bell rang. *San Luis II* pitched down. Her propeller churned, knifing the submarine through the water and toward the deep.

7: JOUST

"No lance have I, in joust or fight, To splinter in my lady's sight; But, at her feet, how blest were I, For any need of hers to die."—John Greenleaf Whittier

The South Atlantic looked like molten gold as the last rays of the sunset illuminated its gently rolling surface. A bubble rose, disturbing the tranquility. And then the bubble popped; foam erupted in its place. From within the eruption, a grey cylinder was spat. It leapt to the air, peeled apart, and opened like a flower. Inside hid a Klub anti-ship missile, an export version of the Russian Novator 3M-54, generally known by its NATO designation: SS-N-27 Sizzler.

Released from its watertight container, the Klub's booster ignited and pushed it into the sky. Small wings unfolded and control surfaces adjusted. The Klub nosed over, leveled, and began to race across the sea. Near where it had sprung, sprang another such bloom. It, too, left the petals of its water-tight canister afloat. They lingered for a moment and then, sucked under, disappeared. As the canister petals fell toward the bottom, they passed two ropes of bubbles where *San Luis II*'s super-cavitating torpedoes had sped.

Torpedoes are named for 'torpor'—a state of lassitude imparted by marine electric rays—and these Russian-made weapons were ready to deliver such a state prior to consuming their prey. The Squalls had been spit from the submarine's hull. Their mid-body fins snapped open and with a pop, rocket motors ignited. Gases emerged from the conical cavitators at the weapons' tips and bubbles formed around the casings, reducing drag and turning the Squalls into underwater rockets. The weapons then charged through the water as though it were air, quickly reaching 200 knots as they raced toward *Dragon*. Swaddled in their self-created gaseous atmosphere and practically tasting the coming kill, the Squalls anxiously screamed through the water.

Some 150 meters below the Squalls, two Type 53-65KE heavy wake-homing torpedoes snaked their way through the darkness. They had been released first, pushed from the *San Luis II*'s tubes by high pressure air and spat into the ocean. The export version of the Type 53 heavy torpedo used HTP—a concentrated solution of hydrogen peroxide. Once a catalyst was introduced, HTP decomposed into a high-temperature mixture of oxygen and steam. The oxygen allowed the weapon's kerosene turbine to breathe, with the steam vented outside the weapon's casing. This made the '53 a high-speed threat, and added to the torpedoes wake of bubbles, created lots of noise. (It also made the weapon very dangerous should it start-up in the submarine's tube.) Western navies had abandoned HTP as a propellant for this very reason. Despite these worries, however, *San Luis II*'s '53s worked as they should, and their contra-rotating propellers accelerated them to some 44 knots. All the while, the sensors in the torpedoes' noses got to work.

Designed to snake back and forth within the vee presented by the wake of an enemy ship, the '53s would approach a target, and when proximate, explode. *San Luis II*'s '53s hunted as designed, running straight and true toward the hunk of steel they were programmed to hunt and kill: HMS *Dragon*. They fell in behind the destroyer and began their meander up her wake.

In the pitch black beneath the ruckus of missile and torpedo launches, *San Luis II* was pointed down in a crash dive. She had released a second noisemaker and would soon pass 180 meters, the depth at which *San Luis II* had released her wake-homing torpedoes.

"Enemy torpedo at three-zero-zero degrees. Bearing: one-zero-three degrees. Weapon is diving. Rapid change in bearing and depth indicative of a helical search pattern," *San Luis II*'s sonar technician reported. "Screw pitch suggests it's a Stingray acoustic homing light-weight torpedo."

"Hotel 1," Ledesma added. "The Merlin..."

"Bow planes at 20 degrees," a voice came from the shadows of the Control Center.

"Two hundred fifty meters. I am headed for 300 meters," another added.

"Sir, batteries now at nine percent."

"*Mierda*," Captain Matias mumbled. Three decks down, in the confines of the battery deck, Raton scurried about on his sled. Using the hull's down angle, he slid along over the tops of the battery cells, braked over the bank that had been soaked by salt water, and locked his sled in place. The last of the water had drained into the bilge and then into one of the boat's starboard tanks. He made his way to the shunt and, swallowing hard, snapped the disconnect switch.

"Sir, batteries back at 17 percent" shouted a voice from above.

"Bravo, Raton," Ledesma stated, with a pump of his fist.

BANG, *San Luis II* complained.

"Approaching three hundred meters."

"Planes to five degrees."

"Aye, sir, my planes are at five degrees down," the planesman reported.

THUNK. CRACK. Everyone except Ledesma and Matias squirmed as *San Luis II*'s high-tensile steel shell adjusted to the squeeze of the ocean.

"A deadly hug," Matias quipped with a crooked smile.

"Three hundred."

"Planes to zero. All stop, both turbines," The captain ordered. Ledesma echoed the words.

"Answers all stop, sir," said the helmsman.

Captain Matias looked around the confines of *San Luis II*'s Control Center. *Our tomb.* He studied the red-lit tangle of wires, pipes, dials, and lights. Matias cursed the narcissism of those who believed they had all the answers. He swore at the sociopathic tendencies of his leaders—the leaders that had ordered him to engage in this folly—and he cursed those who had sent his son to death. As these thoughts played out in his mind, his outward appearance remained one of steadfastness and professionalism. *San Luis II*'s forward momentum stalled, and the boat hung in the pitch-black stillness. The sound of trickling water confirmed that ballast was pumped into a stern trim tank. Matias glanced at the bubble: The boat stayed level in both pitch and yaw.

"Sonar?" he asked.

"Sir, Delta 1 is at zero-two-zero. Bearing: two-zero-zero and turning. Range: 500 meters. Delta 1 has reduced speed, making turns for about seven knots. Enemy torpedo is approaching our noisemaker." A muffled thump sounded somewhere over their heads. "Enemy torpedo has detonated."

"Yes," was hissed by several of the submariners.

At and below the surface, the sub's weapons approached the British guided-missile destroyer.

◊◊◊◊

The Klubs darted in low and fast, skimming just above the water. Kingfisher 21's pilot had spotted their tail-fire on the rippled water. Seamus contacted *Dragon*, reporting his own position lest he, too, be engaged by the destroyer. The helicopter was ordered to gain altitude and hold, so Seamus brought his aircraft up high and banked off to a designated block of airspace. In the meantime, *Dragon*'s air defense radar had already detected the Klubs' cylindrical bodies. The AWO reacted.

"Radar contact. Probable targets," the Op Room had announced over the bridge's Voice User Unit. "Fast movers at two-zero-zero degrees. Bearing: zero-two-zero."

Lieutenant Commander Williams sounded an alarm bell and, with a nod from Captain Fryatt, ordered the wheel hard over so *Dragon*'s bow pointed down the missiles' flight-path, presenting minimum aspect. *Dragon* slowed as well, reducing the turn of her shafts, and thus reduced her self-generated noise.

The captain ordered up the Surface Ship Torpedo Defense System, "Deploy SSTDS." From *Dragon*'s transom, a drum winch paid out a towed array.

Captain Fryatt closed his eyes for a moment, and in the blackness felt the heat and burning smoke from that terrible day aboard *Sheffield*. He remembered the wind in the dark passageway as the fire sucked air, gobbling the air as the fire grew in intensity, choking men with fumes, smoke and oxygen starvation. Fryatt opened his eyes again, but still saw the big round eyes of the sailor in the respirator who had saved him from asphyxiation. He blinked the images away and focused again on the here and now.

Two cell covers popped open among *Dragon*'s forward vertical launching system.

"T-mark for function," Williams spoke to the Op Room by VUU.

"Electric firing selected," Op Room responded.

"Firing granted," Fryatt authorized and Williams repeated.

"Standby."

A deafening bang and a plume of efflux exited the chimney. An Aster 15 leapt from its launcher cell. The dart-shaped missile rose on a fountain of fire that bathed the bridge in an eerie orange glow.

"Good away, one" Williams said as the bridge crew watched the missile climb out.

BANG. WHOOSH.

A second Aster departed.

"Good away, two."

Both missiles climbed briefly, turned over, shaped their trajectory, discarded the booster stage, and dove toward the water.

Nearly simultaneous with the first shot, *Dragon*'s Seagnat Control System had scrutinized wind direction and speed, threat direction, threat range, threat type and the ship's direction and change of heading. It then selected launcher two, and sent three Mark 214 seduction chaff canisters skyward. Pushed away by a low-g rocket, the canisters burst and dispersed clouds of metallized plastic strips.

In *Dragon*'s Op Room, a red light blinked on the sonar station console. The SSTDS's passive towed array had sniffed something and presented it to a midshipman's screen in the Op Room.

Dragon's sonar technician leaned in and scrutinized his display. The midshipman donned his earphones and heard a hiss like steaks just turned on a hot grill.

"Bloody hell," he bounced in his seat, and, turned to the director, proclaiming: "Torpedo, torpedo, torpedo." As those around him shifted their focus from the radar's plan position indicator to sonar readouts, the sonar technician began the classification and identification routine.

Within seconds, he had weapon types to help the director and captain defend the ship: "VA-111 Shkval super-cavitators. Two inbound, bearing zero-two-five degrees." Two more frequency lines appeared on the sonar display.

The midshipman squirmed in his seat again and began to analyze bearing, frequency, and range of the threats.

The Asters dove on the anti-ship missiles. One Aster detonated above a Klub and sprayed it with steel cubes. The damaged Argentine sea-skimmer wobbled and then tore itself apart by dynamic pressure. The second Aster detonated proximate to the second Klub anti-ship missile, but its warhead's shotgun effect missed the target. This second Klub accelerated and broke the sound barrier with a crack as it carried on toward *Dragon*.

"ASM inside outer fence," Williams noted. "Phalanx online. Then the lieutenant commander reiterated: "All weapons free."

Fryatt's only response was a clenching of his teeth that made his cheeks poke out. He looked to the clouds of chaff that floated down toward the sea.

The anti-ship missile screamed over the water and flew at the shape its nose radar said was an enemy target. However, *Dragon*'s chaff made this shape larger than her true mass represented, and the missile's computerized brain continued to adjust its path at what it believed to be the enemy's center of mass. This center, however, was now off to the starboard of the British guided-missile destroyer.

Mounted to its sponson was *Dragon*'s close-in weapons system. With its distinctive radome—nicknamed 'Dalek' after the aliens in Doctor Who—the Phalanx scanned the sea with its search subsystem. When it had found a target and provided altitude, bearing, heading, range, and velocity information to its computer, the computer analyzed the target's range, speed and direction. A millisecond later, the Phalanx swiveled on its mount and raised its Vulcan six-barreled Gatling cannon. Its track antenna and subsystem scrutinized the target, observing it until it determined the probability of a hit was worth firing. On automatic, the computer pressed the trigger, and with a ripping sound the Phalanx spat 75 tungsten bullets per second, walking them into the radar return it had deemed threatening.

Too close for comfort, the remaining Klub anti-ship missile blew up in a flash of orange, black, and red. Its turbojet engine, the most robust part of its structure, splashed in and cartwheeled for a moment before it stopped with a slam and then abruptly sank.

Fryatt sighed and exhaled a breath he had held for minutes. His blued air-deprived face turned pink again, and he turned his attention to the report of underwater contacts. The enemy had reached up to assault them from the air, and now stabbed from beneath the waves. His enemy would try to stick the knife in, twist it, and look into his very eyes as he spilled Fryatt's guts. Fryatt, in that moment and without knowing him by name, respected Argentine Navy Captain Matias. He was, after all, just a patriot doing everything within his power to win. Fryatt nodded. As he acknowledged the existence and purpose of his foe, Fryatt decided he would win, and that he would damn his enemy's shadow to a deep, cold, black grave. But he would do so with a salute and a memory he would hold as long as he lived.

If my life is to be a long one, Fryatt pondered as he looked around at the young people manning his ship's bridge. He loved every one of them. He would never tell them this directly, but had anyone been looking, his usually cold blue eyes would have betrayed the feeling. Fryatt refocused.

"Williams. Squall."

"Sir," Williams turned and as though in a trance, robotically rattled off all he knew about the Russian fish: "VA-111. High-speed. Straight runner. GOLIS navigation system. Preset target information." This last bit was enough for Captain Fryatt to relax.

"Come to heading one-eight-zero. Increase speed: 20 knots," he ordered.

Though the Squall was a fearsomely fast weapon, it ran in a line and was therefore a mere distraction to a highly maneuverable vessel like *Dragon*.

Distraction from what?

"Torpedo, torpedo, torpedo," was the Op Room's answer to his query.

Fryatt raised his binoculars to watch the lines of surface bubbles as the Squalls sped along. When certain they would come nowhere near, he shifted his attention.

"What have you got, Charlie?" Fryatt asked over the bridge phone.

The Op Room sonar technician had localized the other slower torpedoes, and matched their acoustic signature to Type 53-65 heavies. *More Goddamn Russian fish.* He reported to the director, who in turn answered the captain.

Williams' big eyes asked the question as Fryatt hung up.

"Wake homers," the captain said. Everyone on the bridge turned and peered astern as if they could look through steel bulkheads.

Part of *Dragon*'s Surface Ship Torpedo Defense System, a stern-mounted reel, paid out a float and line. The float created a second wake behind the destroyer and began to emit sounds like those generated by an 8,000-ton ship powered by loud engines.

San Luis II's heavy torpedoes had already turned into the vee of *Dragon*'s foamed wake, and had begun to snake back and forth within it. *Dragon* increased speed and started a turn. As she did so, the towed float slowed. This allowed one of the torpedoes to catch up. The weapon armed its 700-pound warhead. Just a few more feet of travel and the torpedo exploded. A geyser of white water rose from the ocean, and the explosion's pressure wave smacked the ship on the ass. The second torpedo continued its advance.

The weapon nibbled at the edge of *Dragon*'s wake, and no longer swimming side-to-side, accelerated. In the Op Room, the technician heard the insect-like buzz of its high-speed propellers drawing nearer. He informed the director leaning over his station. The director rang the bridge.

"Increase to flank. Hard right rudder," Fryatt ordered.

Dragon's bow rose as she hastened and leaned hard in the turn. Fryatt watched as the bow swung around and pointed back at the ship's wake.

"Meet her," the captain ordered.

"Very well," answered the conning officer as he used opposite rudder angle to stop the turn.

"And, rudder amidships."

The ship cut across the wake's consecutive waves and frothy center, slicing through without so much as a bounce. As soon as *Dragon* had cut through the calm lather, Fryatt yapped another command: "Hard left rudder."

The bow swung again, and the hull leaned hard. Sailors grabbed hold of bulkheads and consoles to steady their stance. With a smacking, the ship crossed the wake again and finished the last loop of a large figure-eight she had drawn upon the sea. The torpedo had done its best to turn with the wake. It pierced the outer wave created during the ship's last turn and its nose sensor scanned the area ahead, finding nothing but open, featureless ocean. It would run until its kerosene and hydrogen peroxide were expended. As *Dragon* became a fleeting black shape on the star-lit horizon, the torpedo sank into the abyss.

Fryatt leaned toward Williams.

"How's the Merlin's fuel state?"

"At least another hour."

"Load out?"

"One Stingray and two Mark-11s."

"Excellent. Get me a sonar fix on this bastard."

"With pleasure, sir," Williams responded and powered up *Dragon*'s active sonar.

8: CALOR

"Death makes men precious and pathetic. They are moving because of their phantom condition; every act they execute may be their last; there is not a face that is not on the verge of dissolving like a face in a dream."—Jorge Luis Borges

WHOMP.

The lash of sonar meant one thing: the British destroyer was alive and well.

"Here we go," Ledesma muttered.

WHOMP.

San Luis II shivered. Matias felt her tremor as he leaned against a pipe. He wondered if it was he or the boat that was full of fear. He let go of the pipe, felt the vibration again through his rubber-soled shoes, and looked at his trembling hand. *It's both of us.*

WHOMP.

"Splash," the sonarman stated. "High-pitched screws. Torpedo in the water. It just went active."

"*Mierda*," Matias muttered to himself. One submariner made the sign of the cross as high-pitched pings reverberated through the water. The sonarman squeezed his headphones tight against his ears, and added: "High rpm turbine."

"Hotel 1. The British helicopter," Ledesma breathed contemptuously.

Matias grunted acknowledgment, and rattled off: "Planes up five degrees. Make your depth 250 meters, increase speed to five knots. Ready noisemaker." The captain's voice had become gravelly, betraying his fatigue. Ledesma wondered about the last time the captain had slept, or for that matter, eaten. Ledesma rubbed his own growling belly. He thought about a steak or a nice piece of fish. When he remembered the canned and frozen slop that came out of *Numero Dos'* galley, Ledesma refocused.

"Five knots. Coming up on two-five-zero," he announced to the Control Center.

Matias nodded. "Planes to zero." *San Luis II* leveled again. The submarine's casing creaked with the change in pressure. "Power?"

Seeking an answer for his captain, Ledesma went to the electricians mate. The electricians mate read his station's gauges. He then looked at Ledesma, shrugged, and frowned. Ledesma checked the battery read-out for himself, sighed, and returned to the captain.

"Sir, batteries are down to nine percent." Ledesma paused and exhaled with worry. "We are going to have to--"

Raton heard the protests from the hull. He thought he even saw the secondary inner hull flex for a moment. He, too, lacked sleep and food, and began to doubt his own senses. Raton had nursed the batteries as best he could; shifting leads from terminals, whiffing ozone as they sparked, and topping-off cells with distilled water. Despite such efforts, the available charge was finite and fleeting. *Like life*. The boat answered his thoughts with a sickening groan.

San Luis II had been pushed to her limits. The submarine's steel had been compacted, flexed and stretched.

Her energy was nearly expended. Her oxygen generators and carbon dioxide scrubbers were near empty. Raton's thoughts became clouded and his vision, wavy.

Raton knew the poisons emitted by machinery and the crew's breaths were generally heavier than most gases, and tended to settle within his part of the boat. Raton was, in effect, *San Luis II*'s canary in a coal mine, and the troubles he began to experience confirmed that they had all been underwater for too long. Raton's sled had a growler that could plug in at multiple points along the battery compartment's track. He considered using it.

Raton would beg whomever answered to come to their senses and get to the surface for air, for the opportunity to run the diesels and feed his batteries. His hand trembled as he felt the growler's box. He tugged at its coiled umbilical, fondled its plug, and considered the words he would have for the idiots 'upstairs.' Then he remembered his training and his reverence for *Capitán Matias* and *Teniente de Fragata Ledesma*; his superiors. *Are they superior?* Raton wondered, and then shook his head to clear it. He realized his heart was racing. His studies and training flashed into his mind:

Hypercapnia, from the Greek *hyper*, for 'above,' and *kapnos*, meaning 'smoke.' The condition is one of abnormally elevated carbon dioxide—a gaseous product of the body's metabolism normally expelled via the blood and through the lungs. Raton giggled, and said: "It's true. It's true." A floating head appeared before him. If Raton could have recognized its features, he would know the face belonged to a boy who had died during *San Luis II*'s shakedown cruise. The face smiled and said: "Yes, it is true." Then its smile faded and the face became grim and drained of color. Its dark eyes became sad. Raton's smile faded, too. Then he yelled in horror.

Raton shimmied along to a locker door. He fumbled at its latch and got the locker open. Inside was a diving lung; a bag and mouthpiece the *Rusos* had designed to filter bad air. Raton bit down on the foul tasting bit, slipped the piece on his nose to pinch his nostrils shut, and sucked a lungful of rubber-tasting air. A few filtered breaths later, his head began to clear. He moved along to the growler.

Raton lifted the oversized telephone's connection wire, found the plug at its end, aimed for the receptacle labeled 'Control Center,' plugged it in, and cranked the growler's ringer.

"*¿Sí?*" came over the receiver. Raton sobered himself, as though he were dismissing the effects of a night of drinking Fernet and Coca-Colas.

"*Señor*," Raton said, unsure of with whom he spoke. "*Dióxido de carbono…*"

Ledesma slammed the Control Room growler down. He felt his own balance momentarily waver as he moved to check the environment control panel. The panel's gauges confirmed Raton's report.

"Captain, scrubber efficiency reduced. Carbon dioxide levels are on the rise," Ledesma stated to the captain, who displayed a blank and distant look. Ledesma looked around and saw everyone was breathing harder. He turned back to the captain, gasped, and insisted: "Sir…"

Matias shook his head and blinked hard and fast.

"Yes, Santiago…"

"Captain, we have to get to periscope depth. We have to vent the boat."

Everyone within earshot turned away from their Control Center station panels and looked at Ledesma. They all knew that the surface was too dangerous with a destroyer and a helicopter around. Coming shallow to extend the snorkel would be tantamount to suicide. Captain Matias clenched his fist and struck it against steel. *To have a nuclear boat*, he wished silently. *To run silent and run deep; to be free of the surface and air.* In that moment, Captain Matias understood why his son had died, why Buenos Aires had pushed the boundaries of its industrial and scientific capabilities to acquire such a capability. As certain as he was about his tactics and boat, the inherent limitation of the diesel-electric submarine were fatal if a tin can like this British guided-missile destroyer persisted in its pursuit. Captain Matias collected himself, cleared his throat, and spoke out:

"*Es un día de lealtad.*"

"¡*Sí, mi capitán*!" came back from the men in yelled unison. For it was a day of loyalty, and they would follow their captain, fight their boat, and honor their country, no matter the cost.

"Very well…" Captain Matias strolled the Control Center. He looked at each submariner at their station, patted the shoulder of some, and then ordered: "Diving lungs for all. Those off duty to their bunks.

"Aye, sir," came back, and the men reached into station lockers to pull out and don their masks. Though Matias stretched his over his head, he left it dangling from his neck.

"Launch noisemaker. Planes up 20 degrees. Make your depth 100 meters. Ready tubes one through six for firing," Matias continued.

With a devious child-like grin, Ledesma repeated his captain's orders. With a subtle swish, a noisemaker was released to the water. Most would have paid the sound little mind, though some aboard discerned and recognized the small cylinder's din. Regardless, they all hoped the enemy torpedo would be lured away. *San Luis II* rose in the water column and accelerated, leaving the noisemaker between her last position and the British helicopter-launched weapon.

Matias' eyes rolled in his head. He was on the verge of passing out, he realized. He pawed at his mask, placed it over his nose and mouth, and sucked a few breaths through its round filter element. Lowering the mask again, he exhaled and asked: "Sonar, position on Delta 1?"

"*Señor*, I have Delta 1 at three-three-one; bearing: one-three-two. Speed…" the sonarman paused to confirm his count of blade and shaft turns, "is 11 knots."

"Weapons: firing point procedures, Delta 1. Snapshot, tubes one through four. Reload with ASMs."

Men scurried to make the captain's orders happen. They locked the enemy's position into fire control, programmed the heavy wake-homing torpedoes with those numbers, and prepared four Klub anti-ship missiles for loading. *San Luis II* angled up, making these tasks an urgent uphill coordinated dance. The submarine shuddered, and with a continuous whoosh, four torpedoes were loosed to the water.

"Santiago, bring us in as close as you can. Slam Klubs and '53s down that *mal parido*'s throat," Matias cursed. "Then, surface the boat."

Ledesma hesitated. His usual reiteration of orders—a seeming echo of the captain's voice—was not immediately forthcoming. Then, he finally repeated what had been said. When he did, the captain added:

"Prepare conning tower team for SAM deployment."

Ledesma stood erect and acknowledged right away: "Aye, sir."

Despite the lack of need to salute aboard ship, Ledesma snapped one anyway. The gesture was interrupted by a high-frequency pinging.

"Dipping sonar at zero-nine-eight."

WHOMP, came the low frequency slap of *Dragon*'s bow sonar.

"Active sonar," *San Luis II*'s sonarman reported the obvious. Then he scrutinized the other sounds in the water and reported: "Enemy torpedo approaching the noisemaker." The sonarman fell silent and listened hard, closing his eyes to do so. A moment later he added: "Torpedo has reached noisemaker." The sonarman rocked back and forth, as though the motion would improve his hearing and concentration. He amended his report by saying: "Torpedo has passed noisemaker. No detonation. Torpedo continues to search at two-four-two; depth: 285 meters."

"Make your course--" the captain started.

"Splashes," the sonarman interrupted. His report did not continue with 'active sonar' or 'screws,' which meant:

"Depth charges," Ledesma guessed out loud.

Two Mark 11 depth charges had dropped from the hovering helicopter, splashed in, and began to fall through the water. As they did, the thump of Kingfisher 21's rotors were muffled by the water as the weapons sank. The cylindrical British weapons descended toward their detonation depth: 180 meters, the last depth at which Master 1—*San Luis II*—had been localized on active sonar.

When a depth charge detonates, the high explosive undergoes a rapid chemical reaction. A very high-pressure gas bubble expands rapidly, and creates a primary shockwave that is lethal to man and machine, especially if the weapon explodes in close proximity. Then, as the weight of the surrounding water forces the bubble to contract again, pressure within the bubble builds and causes it to re-expand, propagating another shockwave. This cycle continues until the gas bubble can vent to the atmosphere. It was these cyclical secondary shockwaves that Captain Matias and his crew feared, as they could bend a submarine's hull back and forth until a catastrophic hull breech occurred.

"Make your course one-eight zero," Matias ordered. His plan was to turn the boat in a wide circle and move her to the surface; all in hopes of avoiding this new peril.

"Enemy torpedo circling at two-nine-zero meters," the sonarman added. The Stingray was in an automated circular search pattern. Matias used this information to deprioritize the threat the enemy weapon presented. Knowing the Merlin's weapon load out, the captain rationalized: *If we can bleed this helicopter dry, have it expend all its weapons and send it home sulking, then the destroyer will be vulnerable.* After these thoughts, Captain Matias spoke again:

"Planes to five degrees. Slow your rise. Come to new depth: eight-zero meters."

"Aye, sir, planes to five degrees. Coming to new depth: eight-zero. Repeat: 80 meters. Forward compartment reports tubes one through four loaded with

ASMs. Tubes five and six loaded with Type 53 heavy torpedoes."

"Very well, Santiago. Very well."

San Luis II leaned as she turned a great circle and spiraled upward to the surface. Her crew waited as the depth charges fell through the water in their direction. Despite the submarine's steel skin, the crew's eyes all looked up as if they could see through metal and water and see the descending depth charges. Perhaps they gazed to the Heavens and to God, begging for salvation and maintenance of life… If luck was with them, the enemy weapons would be far off their mark. Some prayed. But even though God hears all prayers, sometimes the answer is 'no.'

A depth charge detonated just several meters behind and below the submarine. The explosion's high-pressure gas created a bright sphere in the black ocean, a small sun that momentarily illuminated the abyss, and then shrank and blackened. The circular shockwave it created slammed into *San Luis II*, shaking her violently. Inside the submarine, lights shattered, panels sparked, fuses blew, and men screamed.

"Left full rudder. Ahead full," Matias shouted.

BLAM. Another explosion.

This explosion was closer and it was big. The primary shockwave was bone-shaking, but then it mixed with the secondary one. Both waves merged, conspired, and crashed into *San Luis II*.

The submarine quaked, rocking back and forth, and wailed like a tormented ghost. Metal tore and men screamed. Those standing seemed to jump in place, and those seated in chairs rose into the air before falling back upon their bottoms. Some men tumbled over as they crashed back down, and the entire boat seemed to flex as though constructed of a green spring twig.

The depth charge's gas bubble shrank and grew again. It slammed against *San Luis II*'s stern. It grabbed her and twisted her. The explosion lifted *San Luis II*, shoving her hard, and pushed her nose down. Then occurred a third explosion. This one felt as though it was right up against the submarine's keel.

Raton was lifted from his sled. His back slammed against the compartment roof. He swore, "*¡Esto es un quilombo!* There was a gush as a battery cell cracked open and spilled its contents in a wave that sloshed along the floor before draining to the bilge. The lights in Raton's little dungeon flickered. He remembered a lullaby from childhood: '*Qué linda manito*'…

Little Gaston Bersa lay snuggled in his bed, beneath thick blankets and cool comforting sheets. He looked upon his father's candle-lit, bearded face. Raton held his hand up. He looked upon the face. It swirled in the carbon dioxide-poisoned haze. Despite the respirator's mouthpiece being jammed against his tongue, he began to hum the lyrics:

Qué linda manito que tengo yo

Linda y bonita que Dios me la dio.

He thrummed his fingers and thought:

What a beautiful hand I have that God gave me.

Beige blurs, Raton's moving fingers trailed. He laughed. The laugh was hard and gasping, and reverberated up through the steel decks. Someone upstairs heard it, but dismissed it as another hallucination, like the floating face Raton kept seeing, and the sounds of the ocean trying to end his life. Then, when the face reappeared, Raton yelled out: "¡*Dióxido de carbon*!"

Kingfisher hovered near where its last depth charge had splashed in. Off the helicopter's nose, the black blanket of sea rose, boiled, and erupted, sending white water airborne. The upsurge folded over and fell back again as surface waves radiated in concentric circles. In the Merlin's rear cabin, John watched the spectacle and knew that, far below, men were suffering. Though this was John's first experience watching weapons being used in anger, he did not feel angry. Instead, he felt pity and respect for those brave enough to travel and fight beneath the waves, in an environment so alien they may as well have been on the Moon.

◊◊◊◊

"Trim the boat," Matias whispered into the planesman's ear as he helped him off the cold steel floor.

"Aye, sir, trim the boat," the shaken planesman answered sheepishly. Leaning back in his seat, the planesman pushed a mushroom-shaped button, and then again when the indicator showed *San Luis II* was back on an even keel.

Patting the man on the shoulders, the captain turned and announced: "Get me a damage report. And switch to emergency lighting."

Ledesma acknowledged and turned on the backup lights which illuminated the compartment in blue shadowy tones. He then made a general announcement: "All compartments, report damage."

The growler rang. Ledesma, his legs shaking, steadied himself and reached for it. He nodded.

"Forward compartment reports tube five is leaking," he told the captain. "Repairs are underway."

"Starboard stern plane stuck at positive seven degrees," the planesman added after unsuccessfully manipulating his controls.

"Fire control computer is down. I need fuses," the weapons officer pleaded. "I need fucking fuses." Someone ran off to get them.

"Okay. That *pajero* helicopter cannot shit on us anymore. Depth?"

"One hundred twenty meters, sir."

"*Señor*, permission to check forward compartment?" Ledesma was already on the way when the captain offered,

"Yes, Santiago. Go. Go. I need those weapons in five minutes."

Ledesma entered *San Luis II*'s forward compartment. A torrent of seawater was gushing from tube five. Torpedomen struggled as their supervisor screamed the obvious: "Make hatch cover tight. Turn, boys. Turn."

"Push harder," one yelled.

"I'm pushing," was the strain-filled response he got. More grunts as the men tried to turn the hand-wheel.

Ledesma scanned the compartment with the cone-shaped beam of a flashlight.

The soaked men groaned and spat water as they fought to tighten the tube's breech valve wheel and rotate the locking ring that held the breech closed when the tube was flooded. The breech, a slug of steel that had Cyrillic letters embossed upon it, seemed such a small barrier between their small envelope of breathable air, and the vast ocean so full of cold, saline death. The chief torpedoman saw Ledesma and instinctively reported:

"*Señor*, tube is flooded. Muzzle door must be damaged. Locking ring is bent," he shouted in clipped sentences.

Ledesma looked at the small red card on the tube's breech door. It read: 'LOADED.' Worried, Ledesma joined the men in their struggle to reseat the breech's wedges in the rotating locking ring. He grabbed a crowbar from a wall rack and drove it between the wedges and the locking ring's groove. He slammed his weight against the bar to bend the ring and guide the misaligned wedge into the indentation. The crowbar came unstuck in failure. Ledesma let out a cry of pain as it hit him in the chest.

"It's the tripping latch arm. It's bent. I need a hammer," Ledesma said. The word 'hammer' came out as a strange gurgle as water sprayed into his mouth. He coughed hard as someone handed him the tool.

CLANG. Ledesma used the hammer to hit the metal arm that aligned the breech door with the tube's barrel. CLANG. *The Brits will hear that for certain.* But he landed yet another blow against the metal arm. CLANG. The flow of water lessened and then stopped, and the men fell to the flooded floor, exhausted and soaked. Breathing hard, the chief torpedoman patted Ledesma hard on the back.

"*Gracias, señor.*"

Ledesma coughed again, smiled, and set off for the Control Center.

San Luis II's bow tipped up again as her rise toward the surface continued. Ledesma grabbed the tight passageway's overhead pipes and wire bundles as the floor

sloped up. He practically fell against the first bulkhead

before he crouched down and swung through its open hatch

and into the Control Center.

9: VIEW HOLLOA

"As God is my witness, I would rather my body were robed in the same burning blaze as my gold-giver's body than go back home bearing arms."—Anonymous (from 'Beowulf').

The electricians mate snapped in the last fuse and slid back out from under a circuit breaker panel. He looked across *San Luis II*'s Control Center to the weapons officer who stared at the dark fire control panel. Suddenly, the panel lit up like a Christmas tree.

"*Finalmente,*" the weapons officer said as he stood, and reported to the captain: "Sir, fire control computer is back on line."

"*Excelente.*"

The weapons officer turned back to his panel, noticed a flashing red light, thumped it with his finger, and spoke again: "Sir, tube five shows as inoperative."

Ledesma dried his hair with a grey towel that had once been white. He added: "Sir, the tube's breech door was secured. But..."

Matias turned.

"But?" the captain asked.

"...There's a '53 still in the tube. It was powered up when the flooding started. I think the umbilical plug shorted."

"*Carajo.*" No captain wanted to hear that he had a weapon powered-up and stuck in a tube, let alone an HTP-propelled one.

"Fifty meters," a voice penetrated the captain's thoughts. Captain Matias focused.

"Snapshot, tube six, Delta 1," the captain ordered.

"*Si señor.* Snapshot: tube six; Delta 1," Ledesma responded and turned to the weapons officer: "Do it." The weapon's officer pushed a button. With a whoosh, high-pressure air shoved the weapon from the hull. "Tube six, weapon away." The officer started his stopwatch.

"Level the boat at 20 meters. And then fire those missiles," Matias ordered.

Ledesma nodded, turned to the depth gauge, and chanted: "Forty, 30…bow planes to zero degrees, stern planes to five. Twenty-five, 20. Level the boat. Fire tubes one through four, target: Delta 1." Hissing sounds signaled that four Klub anti-ship missile canisters had ejected from the hull. "Missiles away."

"*¿Baterías?*" the captain asked.

"Two percent and falling fast," the electrician's mate reported.

"Prepare to raise the snorkel and engage the diesels. Get us onto new heading: zero-nine-zero, three knots, or best possible speed. And reload tubes one through seven with whatever's left in the cupboard."

"*Sí señor*," said Ledesma.

The submarine pitched and yawed in the turbulence of the surface zone. The water at this depth was disturbed and influenced by the atmosphere, and despite her weight, *San Luis II* felt the power of Earth's atmosphere.

"Ever been sailing?" the Captain asked with a crooked grin.

Everyone in *San Luis II*'s Control Room looked at him. Some had blank stares; some looked worried, others were perplexed by the question.

"*Capitán*," one man spoke up, "I have."

Matias smiled wide. "Where?" he asked.

"Off Puerto Madryn, *señor*. A beautiful boat. She was 12 meters. A Catalina."

"*Si, si,* Puerto Madryn," Matias sighed and closed his eyes. He could see the mainsail, inflated jib, the gentle rise and fall of the hull, and the smell and taste of cool, salted air. "Oh, to be sailing right now."

The submariner recognized the need on his captain's face, stood at his station and continued: "…She was named

Mama Qucha. She was good and strong. She had given us the right of passage, and protected our way. Just like our boat, *señor.* Just like *Numero Dos.*"

Captain Matias again opened his eyes. The man who had spoken was just a shadow in the Control Center's red lighting.

"*Gracias,*" Matias thanked him. "The sea is indeed wondrous. Like all those that sail upon her."

◊◊◊◊

Dragon's bow-mounted sonar detected another submerged object. The multifunction console in the Operations Room alerted the Assistant Under-Water Warfare Officer and began to track and classify the contact.

"Torpedo, close aboard," the sailor yelled out. He scanned the data on his display, frantically adding: "Weapon is active and terminal."

"Brace, brace, brace for impact," the Principal Warfare Officer shouted out when…

◊◊◊◊

An explosion shook the submarine's steel casing. The quaking travelled up Captain Matias' splayed sea legs and rocked his very bones. A cheer went up in the Control Center.

"*Numero Dos es Numero Uno*," Matias bellowed. *San Luis II* seemed to rise in response, sucked up by a wave at the surface that had reached down to the submarine's depth and pulled her bulk along for the ride.

"Report," Captain Matias ordered. The pressing of buttons and whispered conversations went silent.

"*Señor* …" the sonarman inhaled deep and hard. "Explosion. Sound is at one-zero-two: The likely position of Delta 1." The sonarman paused and checked his readouts. "Our torpedo," he added with surety. *San Luis II*'s Type 53 had activated on the outskirts of *Dragon*'s wake and turned in, snaked its way up the frothing line, and blew up when it thought it smelled something metal.

The metal that the torpedo had detected belonged to *Dragon*'s hull, specifically right at the portside 5-Deck where the ship's gas turbines were located. When the weapon's simple computer brain had thought it was just close enough, the weapon had blown. The expanding gases formed a bubble jet that stabbed at *Dragon*, piercing and tearing into her.

"The missiles?" Captain Matias queried.

Ledesma looked at his watch, and said:

"Almost there…"

Dragon's bridge shuddered with the explosion. Fryatt grabbed the arm of his commanding officer's chair to steady his stance as *Dragon* leaned to starboard. She snapped back to an even keel when the computer actuated the hull-mounted stabilizer. Red lights flashed on the officer-of-the-watch's multipurpose console, as well as that which belonged to the navigation position. Someone swore.

"Sir," the officer-of-the-watch spoke up, "RPMs are dropping." His words were accentuated by the sudden lurch of *Dragon*'s hull. It was as if the ship had sailed into thick, soupy water that sapped its momentum. "Captain, Gas Turbine Room reports damage and flooding."

The VUU rang. Williams answered and got a report, passing the information to the captain: "Sir, we have lost port gas turbine. Port alternator and switchboard down, as well."

Dragon began to turn toward the left.

"Reduce revolutions, starboard shaft," Fryatt ordered. "Damage control teams to 5-Deck."

In the Op Room, blips appeared on the Air Warfare Officer's console. They were menacingly close.

"Bridge, Primary. Missile, missile, missile," came over the bridge's speaker. Williams went to the combat systems console and selected the radar display. Four missile tracks sped across the screen like bony white fingers, reaching for the chevron symbol representing *Dragon*.

"Missiles terminal," Williams shouted. Fryatt remembered the last time he had heard that, and thought of *Sheffield* and his lost shipmates. He felt an anger he had not felt in a long time. He swore, and then screamed:

"Turn into them. Get both 'Qs' in-line."

The navigating officer turned the ship to minimize the profile presented to the missiles, and to put the threat in the firing arcs of both the starboard- and port-side Phalanx close-in weapons systems.

"Seagnat," Williams confirmed decoys were also up. "Active and distraction." The system had automatically lofted a jammer round as well as chaff to either side of the ship.

The port close-in weapons system came alive. Its turret swiveled and the barrel rose. A crackling roar and a tongue of flame spat a whipped rope of tungsten rounds at the approaching sea-skimmers.

An explosion close-aboard…

Then another…

Dragon shook.

Fryatt raised his binoculars and watched one Klub turn off center and toward where the Mark 251 active decoy hung on its parachute.

Ripping and vibration announced the second Phalanx lashing out at the inbound Klubs, swatting another of the anti-ship missiles in a massive fireball.

The bright flash filled the bridge. Fryatt winced. Everything looked like an overexposed photograph. Then came- the pitter-patter of shrapnel impacting the ship's masts and superstructure. His eyes cleared, and from the red and orange and black wall of fire and smoke, a white shape emerged.

"Brace," Williams shouted.

The Klub slammed into *Dragon*'s 02-Deck just forward of the ship's funnel and right above the starboard small-caliber gun's platform. It pierced the structure's thin skin and detonated within.

The blast ripped into the forward up-take—the stack where exhaust gasses from the ship's power plants vented. They exploded. The shockwave slammed into the armor of 1-Deck, reflected, and the superstructure burst like a balloon. Hot gases and overpressure travelled forward through a passageway, ripped through the navigation officer's cabin and the combined chartroom, and like an unwelcome guest, entered through the bridge hatch, twisting it from its frame and hinges.

"Blimey," John exclaimed as he saw fire and thick black smoke feather off from the still moving ship. The Merlin orbited at a distance and—out of weapons, low on fuel and unable to land—was relegated to reluctant voyeurism.

◊◊◊◊

Fryatt heard only a high-pitched squeal. He tried to breathe, but his body refused to let him inhale the hot toxic gasses that had filled the bridge. Fryatt coughed and spat out the soot and blood that had filled his mouth. He heard groans and, barely conscious, saw a bloody pile where Williams had last been standing. Fryatt tried to stand, but he folded again when he put weight on his broken leg. His head spun and a black shape filled his vision. For a moment, Fryatt wondered if he was dead.

"Captain. Oh My God," the navigator said as he placed a smoke hood and respirator over the captain's head. He gave Fryatt a gentle shake. "Sir."

"Help me up, Angus."

With a yelp of pain, Fryatt was lifted and dropped into his chair. Angus grabbed a fire extinguisher and sprayed it at several small electrical and material fires. He opened the bridge's outer door, which sucked most of the smoke from the space.

"Firefighting?" Fryatt asked with a cough.

Angus went to a console and checked that the ship's firefighting systems had been activated. They were on, which meant that aqueous foam was being sprayed into burning compartments.

Captain Fryatt lifted himself. The pain in his leg made his head swim. However, he was determined to make it to Williams. He moved along the console until he got to the senior officer's chair and the bloody, burnt mess before it.

"Nigel…" he whispered to his friend, and then asked the navigator for the doctor: "Get the Quack up here."

"Sir, Lieutenant Commander Williams is dead. The doctor cannot help him." He had already checked the first officer, and then moved to each casualty and felt for pulses or respiration. At each mound of scorched flesh and clothing, he only shook his head in dismay. Then he came to the quartermaster, who groaned when prodded. Angus laid him out flat.

"Ventilation…" the quartermaster gurgled, his head still filled with duty. The navigator took the cue and went to the right console. It was still energized and working, so he pushed a button that isolated ventilation. He did not know that damage control teams had already manually done the same thing by spinning baffle and louvre controls, all while they fought fires and worked to rescue the injured. The navigator returned to the quartermaster and propped him against the bridge console array.

Fight the ship, Fryatt's subconscious spoke through the confusion of the situation.

"Aye, fight the ship," Fryatt mumbled.

"Sir?" the navigator and quartermaster asked in unison.

◊◊◊◊

The second explosion had been heard by those nestled inside *San Luis II*. A brief cheer had gone up.

"Raise periscope and snorkel. All start on diesels," Captain Matias bellowed with renewed energy and confidence.

The periscope climbed from its hull well, poked from the submarine's sail, and pierced the surface. Captain

Matias unfolded the periscope's handholds and leaned into its viewfinder. He shuffled around as he spun the periscope.

It was early morning, and the sky was painted purple and orange. The ball of the sun had just peeked onto this side of the world. They had been fighting all night. Another few steps and he spotted the profile of that which he sought.

"There she is," the captain hissed with both contempt and begrudging respect. He settled his view, putting the crosshairs of the periscope's reticle right on the target's center of mass. "There she is."

10: EL PARTIDO

"We didn't lose the game; we just ran out of time."—
Vince Lombardi

Dragon filled the periscope viewfinder, though it
intermittently disappeared behind white-topped hills of
water, reappearing again as a trough passed. Matias saw
thick, billowing smoke that trailed behind the British
destroyer. He clicked the periscope's optics to 10 times
magnification and studied *Dragon*'s form.

At this angle, *Dragon* showed as an abstract sculpture
of angles and towers. When her hull rose over a wave,
Matias saw the bright red anti-fouling paint of her bottom

and the crisp, stark black of her waterline. The sharp point

of her bow climbed until Matias discerned the bulbous sonar

dome. The bow fell and dug in again, sending a fan of white

foam before the British destroyer.

"His Majesty's Ship," the Captain hissed. It was the

first time he had seen his enemy.

"*¿Señor?*" Ledesma had heard his captain say

something, but no clarification was forthcoming.

Instead, Matias centered *Dragon* in the targeting

reticle and, with his hand shaking, pushed a switch that

locked the enemy's bearing and distance into the fire control

computer. *San Luis II* leaned and then rolled back level.

Matias spread his legs apart to form a more stable triangle.

He felt the deck vibrate as the boat's diesels spun up. A

breeze touched Matias' face as a Control Room vent blew in

fresh air. He took a deep breath that tasted of salt and

seaweed, and then turned to his panting men. They, too, reveled in the surface air, filling lungs and cooling sticky faces. As the boat's stale air was displaced, the crew's breaths slowed and deepened. Captain Matias smiled.

"Weapons?" he asked.

"*Señor*, '53's in tubes one and six. Tube five's still jammed," Ledesma reported after peaking at the weapons load-out panel.

"Very well. Surface the boat. Prepare for a surface shot. And get the conning tower team up with Iglas. I want that *chupa pija* helicopter," Matias snarled. "It is time to finish this...on our terms."

Raton had heard and felt the diesels start up. They shook the boat hard and reminded him of the tractor he used to ride in the fields at Salta. The tractor had stunk of diesel fumes and it was hard to steer, making his arms ache and soaking his shirt with sweat from the effort. Nonetheless, despite these complaints, he had loved that '*viejo burro*'— 'old donkey'—dearly. Raton let out a chortle that was as much nostalgic pain as amusement with the memory. He watched the battery charge gauge climb slowly and realized he had done it: He had given his boat, captain, and crewmates the life they needed to stay in the fight. Fresh air reached down into the battery deck. As it reached into his little world, it tickled his cheeks, dried his sweat, and filled his blood with needed oxygen. Raton's weary head cleared.

A squirt of water blown by the morning breeze into a fine mist reflected the sunrise's colors. About it, the sea turned from dark to a light blue laced with white bubbles. Then, a black shape pierced the waves and poked at the air. It was a rectangular monolith. As it grew from the surface, a dark and massive shape came from below, washed by falling water. The long, unnatural island broke the chop upon it. Captain Fryatt imagined he was dreaming, but he soon realized what he was looking at:

"Submarine at the surface," the navigator pointed and yelled.

Fryatt went to the shattered windscreen and looked at the whale-like shape. *The 'white whale' to my 'Captain Ahab,'* he thought, though the shape was in fact deep black. Like a void, a black hole, an alternate universe, it had intruded upon his world. Fryatt quickly scanned the *Dragon's* consoles.

The 114-millimeter deck gun flashed 'inoperative' red and, according to the Platform Management System, most other systems were offline as well. However, thanks to damage control teams, propulsion—specifically the starboard alternator, diesel, gas turbine, and switchboard—showed green, as did steering and stabilizers, chilled water, lubricating oil, and several other subsystems.

"Navigator," Fryatt bellowed as he went to rudder control, "Whatever you can muster, mister, all ahead full."

"But, sir…"

"Make it so," Fryatt harshly restated as he wobbled on his shattered leg.

"Aye, captain." The navigator leaned on the starboard throttle. Despite her injuries, *Dragon* surged, raised her bow, and plowed ahead. Fryatt adjusted the stabilizers and rudders, and did his best to keep the surfaced submarine centered in the bow's breakwater. The ship pulled left. Fryatt countered with full right rudder. *Dragon* ran straight and true again, slamming through the waves and breaking grey water over her forward quarter.

To the last, I grapple with thee... Captain Fryatt quoted to himself.

"Sir, starboard turbine temperature rising fast," the navigator reported.

From Hell's heart, I stab at thee...

"Sir, I have to back off."

Fryatt turned and scowled with a burning fire in his eyes.

Captain Fryatt expertly adjusted *Dragon*'s controls. Her bow, like a harpoon, flew toward the shadow that floated upon the dark green waters.

"For hate's sake, I spit my last breath at thee..." Fryatt muttered. He steered his ship at the smooth blackness of the surfaced Argentine submarine, and in the moment, felt as obsessed as Ahab. A squeak of a chuckle escaped Fryatt's clenched teeth.

The navigator looked to his captain and wondered. He re-checked the redlined turbine temperature indicator.

"Sir…" he insisted. Fryatt did not respond.

"What the hell are they doing?" John asked over the intercom as he watched *Dragon* turn and speed up.

"Damned if I know," Seamus responded as he dipped the Merlin in the direction of the enemy. Despite being unarmed and practically flying on fumes, he succumbed to the same instincts as his captain. Bracing themselves against the movements of the aircraft, everyone on board Kingfisher 21 peered through the windows at the spear of *Dragon* as she now raced directly at the fat, floating cylinder of *San Luis II*.

John raised binoculars and scanned *San Luis II*. He watched as water sloshed, broke, foamed, and ran down the submarine's steel casing. He saw free-flood holes suck in and spit out water. He discerned the outline of hatch openings, and as John panned forward, saw the submarine's massive dive planes slap the surface and sink in a storm of bubbles before they rose again and shed a torrent of white water. John shifted his view back again and settled on the submarine's sail. Among the stowed antennae and periscopes that jutted from it, there was another discernible shape; a decidedly human one.

The Russian Kilo-class submarine had been designed to operate in the frozen wastes of the Arctic north, so the sail's conning station was enclosed and wrapped in Plexiglas windows. Since the station flooded when the boat was submerged, it had become cold and wet and slimy. Men of *San Luis II*'s conning station's detail were up there scanning every quadrant with binoculars. John also saw a small platform where two men could stand abreast and proud of the station enclosure. This is where Raton stood for the moment, a reward from the captain for his diligence and as an escape from the extreme confines of the battery deck.

Though smacked in the face by a thick cloud of fumes that emanated from *San Luis II*'s running diesels, Raton reveled in standing outside. He adjusted his personal floatation device for comfort, scanned his quadrant of the sea with binoculars, and sighed with exhaustion. They had all fought through the long dark night. Now it was dawn. The sky loomed as big as ever, and the rising sun painted it with a vast palette of color. Among the crew on the conning station was a two man air defense team.

Both men wore protective goggles, though one, the 'spotter's,' was in fact the thermal imaging type. The team's 'shooter' removed a 9K338 Igla-S from the sail's waterproof locker. The Igla—Russian for 'Needle'—was an infrared-homing man-portable surface-to-air missile. The shooter hurried to assemble the weapon and test and engage the weapon's battery. Raton felt a tug on his pant leg. His brief time in the cold wind was over. He took one more deep breath and then climbed down from his perch.

The shooter ascended in his stead, and was handed the Igla's tube-shaped launcher, which he rested upon a shoulder. Then the spotter joined the shooter on the sail's perch. The shooter threw a switch on the tube's fore grip, and the weapon came alive with an ominous growl, all while the spotter did a quick sweep of the surrounding airspace. His thermal imaging goggles found a source of heat.

The white glowing blob he saw was in fact the Merlin, its hot turbines and exhaust streams standing out, in the infrared viewer, against the black coldness of the atmosphere. The spotter pointed with a small hand-held flag and, taking his cue, the shooter swung the missile tube in the specified direction. The Igla shrilled when its own sensor found the heat source. The shooter centered the launcher sight's illuminated red dot on the inbound British aircraft.

Rodi saw that one of the men perched atop the submarine had a pole rested on his shoulder.

"MANPAD; MANPAD," Rodi exclaimed. Immediately, the aircraft rolled right and yawed hard. Thumps announced the ejection of flares from the helicopter's fuselage. Straining to brace himself, John looked out the window. A corkscrew of white smoke reached for the Merlin.

Despite the length of the tunnel that led up to the sail's conning station, light, sea-spray and the Igla's propellant smoke still made their way down into *San Luis II*'s Control Center. Though one submariner was green from the rise, fall, and roll of the surfaced submarine, the rest seemed content to be breathing the cold morning air. Captain Matias unfolded the periscope's handholds and leaned into its viewfinder. He spun the periscope until he found the British destroyer again, and then settled his view.

Dragon filled his viewfinder. Captain Matias clicked over to 10 times magnification. The British destroyer's hull reared as she climbed a mountain of water. When *Dragon* settled again, Matias saw the menacing wyrm painted on the sharp point of her bow. Despite thick black smoke that

belched from the jagged wreckage of the destroyer's

superstructure, the ship was moving. *Not as crippled as I*

believed...

The submarine leaned and then rolled back level.

Matias stumbled, and steadying himself, re-centered *Dragon*

in the periscope's reticule. The captain pushed the switch

that locked the target's position into *San Luis II*'s fire

control computer. Without taking his eye from the

viewfinder, the captain ordered: "Report tube load-out."

"*Señor*, tube one loaded with a VA-111; tube two:

Type 53 heavy torpedo; tube three: Klub ASM, tube four is

empty; and, tube five: inoperative though still loaded with a

'53," Ledesma recited.

"Very well," Matias said with a hoarse voice. He turned to his executive officer and shouted: "Surface shot: tubes one, two, and three. Do it now. Finish her."

"Fire control, target is Delta 1. Range: 1,000 meters. Bearing: two-zero-zero," Ledesma called out. He looked at the battery charge read-out. Though the indicators climbed, so did Ledesma's anxiety. *The surface is no place for a submarine.* He pushed the thought and doubts aside. Dials were turned and buttons pushed as the attack unfolded. Matias continued to study his adversary through the periscope.

He saw *Dragon* surge forward. "What is she doing?" the captain asked to nobody in particular. *Dragon* sent up a fan of white foam before her charge. Matias' confidence was reinvigorated by the shake of weapons being spat from *San Luis II*'s hull.

"*Señor*, tubes one, two, and three: weapons are away," Ledesma reported. The lilt of his voice betrayed apprehension and spoke volumes, telling the captain to '*Please* dive immediately.'

"Thank you, Santiago," the captain said calmly as he peeled his eye from the periscope's monocle. Then, leaning back in and cupping the viewfinder again in the arc of his brow, Matias peered out at the sloshing waves and his grey foe.

◊◊◊◊

As Seamus put the helicopter on its side and into a tight turn, John was thrown against the aircraft's rear cabin wall. He crawled to the cabin door and kneeled to peer out through the window.

Leaving a smoky trail, and tracking the heat emitted from the helicopter's engine cowlings, the missile snaked its way for the Merlin.

"Christ," John said as he got himself back in the seat and secured his harness. Then he felt his chest, and was reassured that his flotation vest was in fact on. He knew that, if they survived a missile hit, the helicopter would drop like a rock, and once in the water, sink like one as well. He thought back on his escape training.

They had been put in a mock helicopter cabin suspended over a cold pool. It fell and flipped upside down and filled rapidly with the pool water. 'Check your bubbles,' they had told the trainees. 'Bubbles always rise. Just follow them up and out.' John's harness had opened—apparently, purposefully—and he rolled from his seat and hit his head. The cloud of blood that gushed from the wound made it hard to see bubbles, let alone anything else. The other trainees were blinded by it too, as one man swam right into John's face, adding to the throbbing pain. Panic threatened to overtake John's rational brain.

The air in his lungs rapidly ran out, and the organs begged to be refilled. He exhaled the last of the breath anyway, and watched the wobbling bubbles rise. Despite his greying vision, John decided the direction the bubbles travelled had to be the true up. He made for the cabin window opening in the upside-down mock cabin. The opening was already devoid of Plexiglas, a convenience that a real-world Merlin cabin would not have offered.

An explosion tore the remembrance of John's experience at 824 NAS away, and brought him back to Kingfisher 21 and its precarious place in the air over the South Atlantic Ocean.

Shoved by the proximate explosion, the Merlin dipped violently. Although the Igla had been lured by a flare, the enemy missile had exploded close by, the force of which slammed into the helicopter's side. John steadied himself and saw that the window had been pitted by fragments. Luckily, they had not had the energy to shatter the thick Plexiglas and penetrate the cabin. Shaken by the danger-close blast, Seamus had to assume that more missiles were on the way and turned and dipped his Merlin hard.

Raton watched the three trails of bubbles that raced from *San Luis II*'s bow. One trail, the one that belonged to the Squall, formed fast and straight, and left the other two behind it. The second trail stopped short, boiled to the surface, and spat a Klub anti-ship missile into the air. It jumped from the sea and, with a puff of black smoke and an unfolding of winglets, leveled and screamed off. The third

trail—that which belonged to the heavy wake-homing

torpedo—made a relatively slow and steady advance toward

their adversary.

From *Dragon*'s bridge, Fryatt saw the Klub broach,

ignite, and configure for flight. He said: "Not this time.

You are just too close." He knew naval weapons like the

back of his hand, and recognized that *Dragon* was already

inside the effective engagement envelope of this particular

type of Russian anti-ship missile. Fryatt shifted his

concentration to the line of bubbles generated by the

underwater rocket reaching out for his vessel. "Squall," he

annunciated with derision, and reduced the ship's rudders'

angle. *Dragon* swung over obediently, and became oblique

to the threat vector. Fryatt dismissed the Squall with a snort, and then neither saw nor worried about the torpedo that still made its devious way beneath the waves. *Out of sight, out of mind*, Fryatt chuckled at the thought. Though deadly, torpedoes were slower than underwater rockets and anti-ship missiles, and Fryatt decided he would deal with it only if he was forced to. He refocused attention on the black bobbing mass of the Argentine submarine.

"Sir, starboard turbine now at redline," cried the navigator.

"Steady on," was all Fryatt said as his enemy loomed ever larger in the bridge's windows. "Steady..."

The navigator took a deep breath to fortify his own confidence, and then took it upon himself to announce to those below decks: "Collision warning. Brace, brace, brace."

Madre de dios, Raton thought. He had never considered he would see such things: His submarine was at the surface and firing on a British destroyer that already trailed black smoke from fatal wounds. *Our captain has done well.* Raton patted the steel of *San Luis II*'s sail. *And you have also done well, too, my dear.* The air defense crew went about reloading their Igla launcher. Raton looked to *Dragon* again. The British destroyer was in motion, and had turned straight at *San Luis II*.

"*Carajo*," Raton muttered. He lowered the binoculars, and picked up the growler. He pushed the button to sound a bell in the Control Room, and then wiggled the wire plug to make sure it was properly seated in the conning station's terminal. *Fucking Russian piece of shit*, he complained, and spoke aloud: "Come on, come on." Raton looked up to see *Dragon* ride up a wave and then slam back down again. "Come on." Growing anxious, he looked up again. The ship was clearly on a collision course. Judging by the bow wave shoved up before her, she had increased speed, too. *"Answer, damn it, answer."*

A voice finally came through. It belonged to the first officer.

"¿Sí, cuál es su informe?" Ledesma asked for Raton's report.

Raton yelled in response: *"Señor*, the ship...she has turned to. She is charging."

The other men on the sail heard Raton's statement, too. First, they looked at Raton, then, turned with swiveling heads to the only shape on the lonely plain of ocean: *Dragon*. They had all been distracted by the engagement with the helicopter—now just a black shape buzzing low on the horizon—and had failed to recognize the threat that

drawing ever closer. The air defense team shooter swore,

slid the reload missile and launcher back into the sail locker,

and anticipating a dive, clamped the locker door shut.

Within *San Luis II*'s Control Center, Ledesma

informed the captain of the lookout's warning. Matias took

a quick peek through the periscope, and conceded that

Dragon's course and speed were alarmingly uncharacteristic

of a fatally crippled vessel. There was a brief debate

regarding British capabilities and intentions, and then Matias

reluctantly barked the order: "Emergency dive." Ledesma

sounded the alarm and ordered the sail team to get below.

Raton hesitated for a moment. All had seemed well.

Victory had been at hand, and the very reason for his service

and suffering had been vindicated. And now, he was told to

scurry back down a hole. *I am to be a rat that runs for*

cover. Raton scowled, unplugged the growler, and told the men of the watch to get below. As the point of *Dragon*'s bow stabbed closer, and the tower of her superstructure made shadows where none had existed before, Raton's crewmates scurried to the sail's hatch and circled it like confused birds. The opening was so small, and the pressure hull's access tube was so tight, that precious moments were spent squeezing inside and shimmying down. The ladder inside the confines of the access tube was coated with water and salt. It was slippery like the slope of the sail's hull.

Raton huffed. "¡*Señores*! ¡*Rápidamente*!" Raton urged his crewmates to hurry. If the moment had not been urgent, Raton would have laughed as he watched the men try to shove themselves inside *San Luis II*'s hull. *We are all just 'rats.'*

The last of the sail team—a robust and rotund type—
tried to squeeze into the hole, but got stuck as the ring of fat
about his midsection caught on the portal's circle of steel.
Raton directed him to blow out his breath and squeeze in,
and the submariner managed to shimmy inside, disappearing
like a deep-water tube worm entering his enclosure. Out of
breath from pushing on the man's shoulders, Raton saw that
San Luis II's cylindrical hull had angled down, and the
forward deck was awash with creamy bright-green water.
Raton looked to *Dragon*.

A sharp knife at the submarine's throat, the British
destroyer was nearly upon *San Luis II*. Raton wondered,
*Could such determination be defeated? Was such loyalty
paralleled?*

"Close the hatch," was the answer to such questions.
The order had travelled up the access tunnel and been

amplified by its confines. It was Ledesma's voice, a man Raton had admired. However, now, the voice brought abandonment and condemnation.

Several meters down, within the underworld of *San Luis II*'s hull, the primary hatch clanged shut. Its locking mechanism articulated and finalized the situation. Raton felt the submarine tip forward. He was alone. He was outside. *San Luis II* began to dive.

Raton's brain raced: *Had they forgotten him? Was he being sacrificed?* Raton looked up. *Dragon* was just a wall of grey steel. The ram of her prow crossed the patch of foam that *San Luis II*'s hull had just occupied, and Raton looked to the submarine's outer hatch. It was still open, a portal to either salvation or damnation. Whatever the reason for his being left topside, Raton would do one last thing. It would not be for Argentina or his captain, but instead for his boat and fellow submariners. Raton slammed the outer hatch shut. The sound reverberated through his soul and imparted final verification. He had been left topside.

The men he had struggled to give power to, to keep alive, had left him there. Grateful for the air and sea spray, he felt he belonged below where the air was dirty and stale and tasted of battery acid, farts, and sweat. He accepted his place and forced the hatch's locking lever, confirming his position and fate with the metallic ring of steel.

The hatch's lever—half rust, half over-painted metal—broke the finger bones of his right hand as it snapped into position. Raton was unsure whether the scream that came from his mouth was one of pain or resignation to his fate. A spray of cold water refreshed and stung his cheeks, and the sensation both quieted and confirmed the reason for his shriek. It also confirmed that he was still alive. Raton looked up and saw the sharp, grey shape of *Dragon* looming ever larger.

He saw the red wyrm that adorned *Dragon*'s bow. The mythical creature hissed and spat and threatened with razor-sharp claws. The shape rose and fell down almost upon him. There was a deafening crunch and a bone-jarring tremor as Raton was knocked hard to the conning station's deck where he hit his head. The world went black.

Raton tasted salt water and the coppery tinge of blood and realized he was underwater. Light and dark alternated as he tumbled. Bubbles hissed all about him. He tried to struggle toward the light, but the strobe effect continued the eddy created by *San Luis II*'s sinking mass tossed his body like rag doll. Despite his predicament, Raton thought of those trapped inside the submarine.

The Control Center lights had flashed off and on, then off again, and stayed that way. Ledesma reached through the darkness for where the captain had been standing. He felt only cold, wet metal. Unsure of where the floor ended and the rounded walls began, Ledesma probed the dark. He heard groans and coughs and he heard shouted orders. Ledesma added his own cry to the cacophony: "¡*Capitán*!"

"Santiago…" Matias responded weakly.

Ledesma made for the voice and called out: "Someone…give me a flashlight." His hand was smacked by a flashlight, as a surgeon receiving an instrument from an operating room nurse. He grasped the small rubber-covered cylinder and offered to the shadowy figure: "*Gracias*" He clicked on the flashlight. Its cone of light cut the blackness like a knife, and its yellow eye travelled over the dripping control panels, pipes, wires, and valves of *San Luis II*'s

Control Center, and over the fear-filled faces of her crewmen.

As though attempting to pass through, one man held the curved wall of the inner pressure hull. Another submariner was at his station, hunched before the depth gauge, dutifully watching as its needle indicated increasing depth. He turned valves and clicked switches. Despite these efforts, however, the submarine continued to roll farther onto her side, and she pitched steeper and steeper as she slid backward toward the bottom.

As Ledesma's light moved over the submariner's face, the man raised a hand—not as a salute, but a shield from the blinding beam—and with his face expressing resignation, shook his head in the negative. He tried to speak, but instead coughed and spat out the water that had flowed off an overhead pipe and drenched his face, filling his mouth. Then he tried again: "Sir, she won't answer. She--"

San Luis II interrupted her crewman by protesting the abuse she had endured with a bone-chilling metallic whine. The crewman's eyes widened as he finished his thought. "Sir, *Numero Dos*…she is going down." Ledesma exhaled, for he had already known this truth.

"Emergency surface: Blow mains; blow auxiliaries; blow safeties. Planes all down; engines ahead full." With these orders, which were dutifully repeated, but likely with no real hope, Ledesma shifted attention to finding his captain.

The circle of light continued its scan, and it finally found Matias. His face was so bloodied that Ledesma would not have recognized the slumped man as his superior had the flashlight not caught sight of the uniform shoulder board's four gold-braid stripes and looped top stripe.

"*Capitán Matias*," Ledesma stuttered, "*¿Estás bien?*"—'Are you okay?'—Ledesma asked, his voice betraying the deep concern of a man who held his duty to be protective, respectful, and responsible. Against the lean of the deck plates, Ledesma scampered to the captain. Despite a jarring roll from the submarine, he stayed low and made it to Captain Matias. He supported his superior's slumped weight and cradled his bowed head.

"*Señor…*"

"Santiago…" Captain Matias coughed, hocking bloody sputum. "My son…he calls to me. He wants me to come home."

"*Capitán…*"

"*Lo siento mucho.*"—'I am sorry'—Captain Matias forced from his clogged windpipe.

"Sir... You fought well. You have honored us all. You have honored our boat, our crewmates, all of us. I am proud to serve with you, to have served under you. You *are* my captain...always," Ledesma ranted, on the verge of tears.

"The British..." Matias forced. "These Englishmen..."

"*¿Si, señor?*"

"Do not--"

Captain Matias succumbed to his head wound, and died in the arms of his comrade.

Santiago Ledesma was certain that his captain had tried to say: 'Do not hate them. Instead, respect them. For they are just like you: Of Country, of honor, and, of Determination.' Ledesma then remembered a quote from Jorge Luis Borges.

The Argentinian Poet and Essayist had chimed in regarding the first conflict between Argentina and the

United Kingdom—two great, proud nations—over barren rocks. Borges had written: "The Falklands thing was a fight between two bald men over a comb."

With the blood-covered body of his dead captain nestled in his arms, Ledesma laughed like a man under stress, a man who questioned his grasp on the world, and who wondered about the bounds of his reality.

"Eighty meters. Keel: 30 degrees off level. Stern down 22 degrees," someone shouted from the darkness.

"Main tanks have blown." And then, "Machine room reports heavy flooding. Damage control team is in place."

Red emergency lights came on just as the growler rang. The electrician's mate stood before Ledesma, looked to his dead captain, and reported: "Sir, emergency lighting activated." The growler called for attention again. Ledesma gestured, the electrician's mate answered it, and listened intently. His face fell, an expression of desperation replaced by one of hopelessness. He dropped the growler, which bounced up and down on its coiled lead. "Forward compartment reports," he stuttered, "the torpedo in tube 5…its motor has started."

Ledesma bowed his head and closed his eyes, for he knew the inevitable. Less than two minutes later, the jammed torpedo's HTP motor, with its propeller over-speeding, and unable to vent the high-pressure oxygen generated by its chemical reaction, exploded. This triggered the weapon's high-explosive warhead, fatally bursting *San Luis II*'s pressure hull.

Dragon slowed and stopped. She went low at the bow, dipping her head beneath the oncoming waves. The sonar dome and a portion of the stem had been ripped away, and the ship's forward compartments now lay open to the sea and were flooding fast. On the bridge, both Captain Fryatt and his navigator had gone unconscious.

Fryatt had been thrown into a panel and a gash lay torn across his forehead. Angus had slammed into the wheel, fracturing his rib cage and folding him over until his temple impacted a monitor. He was thrown to the floor as *Dragon* yawed hard at the impact. He lay where he landed. One of the snapped ribs stabbed into his left lung, digging deeper with each shallow breath. As life slipped from the navigator, a smashed circuit box sparked and sizzled, kindling a fire.

The Merlin swept in when the bright red of a personal floatation device was spotted cresting a wave. Flying the Merlin into the wind, Seamus approached and slowed the aircraft to a hover.

"Man floating in the water," Rodi announced, judging him to be unconscious or dead. The Merlin's rotor thrust air down in a 70-knot blast that formed a circle of sea foam. Soon the floating shape floated at the center of this circle. "Good position," Rodi confirmed, and slid the helicopter's cargo door open.

John was shoved by salty wind, and the roar of the Merlin's three turbines flooded the rear cabin. In his search-and-rescue capacity, John sent power to the cargo door-mounted rescue hoist just as Seamus activated the Merlin's hover trim controller. He gave thumbs up to Rodi.

Rodi nodded and clipped his safety harness and halyard onto a cabin floor eyelet and then leaned out to grab the hoist arm, slewing it out into a locked position. When it was deployed, the winch paid out several yards of slack cable. Rodi clipped a lift harness to the swivel hook, and then peeked out and down. He saw the man in the water.

◊◊◊◊

Raton came to and looked up at the hovering helicopter. His face was blasted by wind-whipped sea spray that stung his flesh, keeping him conscious.

I am at the surface, Raton thought. He tried to yell out, but his mouth filled with cold salt water that choked him and made him cough and spasm. He recovered a breath and spat the liquid out as the rotor-generated wind continued to smack him in the face. Raton again tumbled under, took in a mouthful of Atlantic Ocean and re-surfaced. He waved his hands and, despite his burning throat, screamed: "¡*Ayuda!*" Most of the cry became an indiscernible gurgle, not that those in the hovering Merlin could have heard Raton anyhow.

"Survivor in distress," Rodi said when he saw the irregular motion of Raton's waving arms within the surging rhythm of dark blue waves and whitecaps. Rodi shouted the announcement to John who in turn used his headset microphone to transmit the information to the helicopter's cockpit. Seamus looked again to the sea's surface, locked his eyes on the bright red personal floatation device that now stood out from the darker background, and dropped his hover another several meters while adjusting it to bring the relative position of the cabin hoist directly above the survivor. Rodi turned to John and gave a thumb's up.

"Good hover," John conveyed to the cockpit.

"Roger," Seamus acknowledged, and then told John: "We're at bingo fuel, so make it fast."

"Understood," John responded. The Merlin again slid in over the sailor's position.

Rodi used a hand signal and John threw a switch on a panel. The hoist cable began to pay out from the winch. Rodi guided the cable down through a cylinder he formed with his gloved hand. Dangling beneath the hovering Merlin, the harness and the cable's weighted end swung in a pendulum effect, lowering steadily toward Raton.

A few seconds after Rodi had signaled to stop the winch, and steadied the cable, he spun his hand in the air. John reversed the winch, hauling in the cable. A moment later, Rodi signaled that the survivor was clear of the water.

"Clear to be banking left," John told the cockpit. Rodi slowly spun one hand in the air as he guided the cable with the other. "Uploading to aircraft at this time." Wide-eyed, soaked and hanging by the harness, Raton appeared in the Merlin's cabin door. "Survivor outside cabin door at this time." Rodi pumped a fist. John stopped the winch and locked it. "Survivor coming into cabin at this time." Rodi hauled Raton inboard and, when he was firmly on the cabin floor, unhooked the lift cable from his harness.

"*Gracias*," Raton sputtered and nodded to both his rescuers. Rodi helped Raton into a fold-down jump seat, secured the safety belt about his waist, and then wrapped him in a blanket, being careful to not further damage his swollen and obviously broken hand.

"Survivor aboard," John told the cockpit. As Rodi stowed the lift equipment and slid the cabin door shut, John unhooked his belt, got up from his seat, and went to the man. Raton coughed up water and John thumped his back.

"*Gracias*," Raton repeated to John and the man in the helicopter's door who did his best to balance against the wind and stow the winch. John spotted the flag on the man's shoulders.

"Argentine? You're Argentine?"

"*Sí, soy argentino; un submarino argentino. Mi nombre es Raton,*" Raton explained he was in fact Argentine; an Argentine submariner.

"Raton?" John asked with a puzzled look on his face, for he recognized the Spanish word for rat. Raton thought for a moment and then offered his real name; the name his mother had given him, not the nickname he had been given aboard *San Luis II*.

"*No, no, yo soy <u>Gaston</u>... Cabo Segundo <u>Gaston</u> Bersa.*"

"Hello, Gaston, I am Juan," John shoved his hand out. "Leading Seaman John Mcelaney, Royal Navy." Raton took the offered hand with his unbroken hand and weakly shook it.

Gaston coughed one more time, expelling the last of the salt water in his lungs, and spat into a small puddle on the Merlin's cabin floor. Rodi, done stowing the rescue winch, knelt down and patted Gaston on the back.

"*Gracias*... Thank you," Gaston offered. Rodi smiled, his mouth a wide arc beneath the helmet's shade. Gaston collapsed against his seatbelt as the helicopter—flying on mere vapors from its tanks—banked hard and raced back to *Dragon*.

Black smoke billowed from vents and openings on *Dragon*'s superstructure as the stopped destroyer corkscrewed in the chop. She was low in the water, especially at the bow, and leaned heavily to starboard. As

Seamus began his final approach, he noticed that one of *Dragon*'s transom closures was ajar, venting a plume of thick grey smoke.

"Draig, Kingfisher 21, requesting clearance to land," Seamus transmitted and waited for a response.

With only static on *Dragon*'s air traffic control channel, Seamus repeated his call. He looked to his fuel and confirmed that both tank indicators had bottomed in the red.

"Sod it," he said, and then changed channels, stating: "Draig, Kingfisher 21, we are landing. FDO, prepare flight deck for landing." *Dragon*'s flight deck officer did not answer, either. Seamus looked to the ship's helicopter visual approach system. Its signal lights were dark. The advanced stabilized glide slope indicator was also off. However, the deck's line-up lights were still illuminated, which meant the seemingly wrecked destroyer had some power available. Seamus used the lights to guide his machine over *Dragon*'s stern. Though he had done this hundreds of times before, Seamus suddenly realized that to land a moving thing on another moving thing was wholeheartedly unnatural. Despite such qualms, he skillfully manipulated the pedals and sticks and began his descent.

Caught by a big wave that travelled down her stricken length, *Dragon* kicked her stern into the air. Seamus got spooked. He increased collective and power, suddenly and fully, causing the aircraft to rise quickly, wobbling. He fought the controls, struggling to come level again. *Dragon*'s stern slammed back down in a whoosh of white foam and spray. The Merlin had avoided being swatted from the sky by 8,500 tons of steel.

BWUP; BWUP, an alarm sounded in the Merlin's cockpit. It was followed by the computer's monotone synthetic voice that warned: "Fuel."

"Tell me something I don't know," he shouted above the thump of the rotors. He manipulated the cyclic between his legs, jockeying the stick left and right and forward and back. His other hand lifted and lowered the collective, while his feet pushed and released pedals that swung the tail left and right. The Merlin drifted over the lines painted on *Dragon*'s flight deck. When he felt the aircraft was centered, he twisted the throttle on the collective, and feathered the blades. The Merlin dropped and slammed into the deck. Its landing gear absorbed most of the shock, but there was still plenty left for those aboard to feel it in their bones. Once certain his aircraft was safely aboard, Seamus began shut-down procedures. He ordered Rodi to secure the tie-down chains and John to check on the ship's bridge.

"Aye sir," John responded and then ripped off his headset, unbuckled from his seat, and slid the cabin door open. He patted Gaston's shoulder.

"Sorry, mate, but we will have to put you somewhere," he told Gaston, who looked confused until Rodi pointed to his holstered sidearm. Gaston nodded and offered a crooked smile of understanding. John jumped out onto the flight deck. It took a moment to find his sea legs. He braced against the pitch and yaw of the ship and then, looking toward the bow, took several wobbly steps in that direction.

There was no way to get forward without going inside Dragon's faceted hull. John opened a gastight/watertight doorway that allowed access to the hangar. He found no personnel there. Moving through another 1-Deck doorway, he entered an air lock that if memory served, after two ladders and hatchways, would allow him access to the ship's main passageway, known informally as the 'Main Drag.' Just as John felt confident he was making progress, he opened a 2-Deck hatchway and a blast of heat and smoke smacked him in the face. Adding to his despair, he saw a dead sailor on the opposite side.

The man had apparently tried to open the door and had run out of air and possibly the will to live. He had slid down the cold, hard steel and formed a lump that seemed to warn: 'Go No Farther.' John gently closed the man's eyes and continued on.

The passageway, smaller than the Main Drag, was dark and smoke-filled. In places, ventilation ducts and water pipes had cracked and fallen when the hull had flexed beyond their limits. John shimmied past them. He felt his way and the heat from the wall. Beyond the steel wall lay the funnel, which meant the space where the engines exhausted was afire or was drawing heat from deeper within the ship.

Dragon, John thought, *my poor, poor old girl.* The ship was now listing hard, and feeling he was moving downhill, it was obvious the bow was heavy. He focused. *I must find the captain.* John persisted toward the bridge.

He found the bridge wrecked, as was the captain, "Sir," John shook him gently. The responsive cough was blood-spewing, but it signaled life. "Sir," he repeated. John cradled his captain and lifted his weight, propping it against the central console. Captain Fryatt groaned and struggled to open an eye. "Easy, now, captain. Easy does it. Do not speak." John went to the communication panel, donned a headset, and tried to contact every compartment. "Damn."

An expended fire extinguisher crashed to the floor from where it had been left on the central console. John watched the cylinder roll forward. He stood and peered through a cracked windscreen and out over the foredeck. It was almost awash. A wave reached up and smashed into the breakwater, dousing the deck gun. He watched white foam cascade off the sides as the bow tried to come back up. It was obvious that the A compartment was flooded, perhaps as high 2-Deck.

"Damn."

In fact, a watertight door separating A and B compartments had been comprised, twisted in its frame, and water was now streaming into the area beneath the missile silos. Despite valiant efforts at both firefighting and damage control by the lads, *Dragon* was going down. As if to accentuate the direness of the situation, the stressed hull let out a groan.

"We yield but to Saint George," Fryatt muttered.

"Yes, sir. 'We yield but to Saint George." John smiled for a moment, then the expression fell into a frown. "I'll get you help, sir." John went to the outer hatch, shoved it open, and screamed for assistance. When he re-entered, Fryatt had slumped back to the floor. John gently lifted the captain's head and felt his jugular. The thump of blood flow was there, though weak. "Damn. Sir? Sir?" *Dragon* shook, interrupting John's doubts. Air rushed from outside as it was sucked down the passageway to the source of the explosion. Then, barely a second later, the ship's interior exhaled through the bridge, and brought its breath of heat and fire and smoke. John was thrown to the floor and Captain Fryatt's body folded and his head smashed against the cold steel deck. John's face hurt and he smelled singed hair.

"Abandon ship, abandon ship," a far-off voice screamed. John crawled to the captain, reached out to feel his neck again, and then saw the severity of Fryatt's head wound. He concluded that the strawberry jam upon Fryatt's cracked head was brain matter. The captain's glazed open eyes reinforced what John already knew. As if to affirm the situation, *Dragon* lurched hard. *Abandon ship…*

John grabbed a floatation device from a locker and made for the exterior hatch. The ship rolled, and John took steps to get outside. He then jumped from the bridge wing into the cold embrace of the sea.

He surfaced and spat salty, sweet seawater. *Dragon* was slipping under. The suction tugged at his legs. John swam away, escaping the downward pull. Geysers erupted from hull openings as air was forced from *Dragon*'s interior. It hissed and howled and rained upon John.

"My poor girl," he whispered, when he looked to the Merlin helicopter chained to the flight deck. As much as he loved his ship, to see the Merlin strapped to her sinking decks was even more painful. *An aircraft at the bottom of the sea*, he contemplated morosely. *Just not bloody natural for a sweet bird to become a reef for fish and slimy things.* He could not watch. He had to turn away. When he did he saw a flash of orange. A life boat.

Gaston leaned over the boat's gunwale, hesitated for a moment when he saw John's burnt hair, missing eyebrows, and the patch of singed flesh that had sluffed from his forehead, and then grabbed hold of his life vest, using his good hand. Another shivering sailor grabbed hold too, and they hauled John aboard.

"Thank you. Thank you."

"*De nada, mi amigo*," Gaston grunted. The effort was nothing for his new friend, for the man that had helped pull him from the cold, slow death threatened by vast open ocean. John flopped onto the lifeboat's bench. As soon as he was up again in the rocking craft, John turned to view *Dragon*.

There was just a triangle of grey metal remaining, and it slipped under quickly. *Dragon* disappeared fast, and was on her way to the bottom. The proud ship left only a boil of light blue water and bobbing flotsam behind. All the sailors in the life boat were silent. Gaston thought of *San Luis II* and his crewmates.

"*Qué pérdida*," Gaston said.

"What's that then, Argie?" a sailor asked derisively.

Gaston thought for a moment and made the attempt:
"A waste."

The sailor considered this for a moment. Then he grunted agreement.

"Contact," the sailor with the binoculars yelled out. "Ships at…" he checked a handheld compass attached to his life vest, "north northwest." The life boat rocked as several men stood at once. John rose slowly and looked where everyone was pointing. He squinted and on the horizon saw two grey outlines. One was clearly larger than the other.

EPILOGUE: WARIAN

"Only the dead have seen the end of the war."—

George Santayana

The Atlantic's mood had turned. She had calmed herself, and her surface reflected this new internal peace. The starry night reflected in the watery blackness, and confused the demarcation between realms. Manships disturbed this newfound state.

His Majesty's Ship *Dauntless*—a Type-45 destroyer and sister of *Dragon*—as well as the Royal Navy frigate *Montrose*, cut their way through the temporary oceanic stillness. They stirred up a creamy white from the deep dark, and reflected the heavens, which danced and whirled in their wakes. With *Dragon*'s survivors aboard, they steamed south by west, and made way toward a rendezvous with an American nuclear attack submarine on a very special mission. *Dauntless* was directed to take up position off the Falklands, and to provide an anti-air warfare umbrella over Stanley and much of East Falkland.

The *Edificio Libertador*—'Liberator Building'— imposed its 20-story shadow upon Buenos Aires' Avenida Paseo Colón. The French Renaissance-style edifice comprised three staggered sections with two wings anchored by a taller central one. Argentina's Ministry of Defense called it home, and connected itself by a tunnel to the president's executive mansion, the *Casa Rosada*. From *Edificio Libertador*'s black mansard roof, the flag of the republic snapped in a stiff breeze, and antennae and satellite dishes poked and pointed at the sky. On the building's lawn, before its columned portico, artillery pieces sat in limbo, and an immobile tank and a statue of a charging soldier. They all stood vanguard among the palms and other swaying garden trees. Deep beneath the structure, below layers of steel-reinforced slabs designed and built to stop the latest piercing bombs, was the War Room.

A man with the weight of the world upon him, Minister of Defense Juan Cruz Gomez scurried from console to console. Each console had screens displaying the disposition of Argentina's forces on the Patagonian coast and the *Las Islas Malvinas* theater of operations. Computer-generated icons represented aircraft at bases and in the sky, ships and submarines upon and beneath the water, and various symbols represented ground forces—companies, brigades, battalions, and divisions. Gomez studied each screen and projected movements in his head, envisioning the checkmate of his enemy. His thoughts were disturbed by an uneasy feeling, and he turned to meet the piercing gaze of Dr. Waldemar Amsel.

In his wheelchair, Amsel was perched on a concrete balcony that jutted over the War Room. He was, of course, smoking; his usual state when his daughter Valeria, the president, was otherwise occupied.

"Where is *Hornero*?" Amsel yelled out, referring to an operative's codename, coughing from the respiratory exertion.

Minister of Defense Gomez craned his neck to look up at Amsel's perch.

"Herr Doctor…" Gomez acknowledged. He leaned over and checked another computer screen. "We are waiting for Major Vargas to check in." Gomez knew that the assassin's last communique had not been confidence-inspiring, but he had failed to mention this in any report to his superior. Vargas' pursuit of the British Crown Prince had become disappointing, so far unsuccessful, and had far exceeded operational schedules. Furthermore, Vargas had failed to report in on time. *Not a good sign*, Gomez thought. It would be another day before he received confirmation that Vargas had failed and been killed, and that the British Crown Prince had escaped. Gomez returned his thoughts to the campaign and the battle that raged on *Las Islas Malvinas*.

Twenty years later…

John Mcelaney strolled Buenos Aires' *Cementerio de la Recoleta*. He passed graves and tombs: those of Eva Perón; past presidents of Argentina; Nobel Prize winners; the founder of the Argentine Navy; and, a granddaughter of Napoleon. John kept the bell tower of the Church of Our Lady of Pilar off to his left as he followed the stone path, breathed in the fresh sea air, and listened to the birds and the breeze rustling the leaves of shade trees. He passed a marker commemorating 1982's *Guerra del Atlántico Sur*. *Turn right at the marker*, he remembered the directions he had been given. The path split and he went right. Emerging from behind a cluster of fragrant, colorful roses, John arrived at the memorial.

There, before the black marble monolith, before the bronze plaque with the outline of the submarine ARA *San Luis II* and the names of her dead officers and crew, he found Gaston Bersa. He was crouched and had his eyes closed in prayer, but when he heard John's footfalls, he stood and turned. A smile replaced his dour expression.

"Juan."

"Hello, Gaston."

"*Bienvenido a Argentina.* Welcome, my friend, welcome." John smiled back and the two men shook hands. Then, they both turned back to the memorial. Only the birds and breeze broke the silence.

29568735R00159

Made in the USA
Middletown, DE
24 February 2016